THE GREYT ESCAPE

MYSTIC'S END MYSTERIES BOOK 5

LEANNE LEEDS

BADCHEN PUBLISHING

The Greyt Escape
Published by Badchen Publishing
14125 W State Highway 29
Suite B-203 119
Liberty Hill, TX 78642 USA

THE GREYT ESCAPE

ONE

"Bella Bailout X Three Peat Ingathered?" Azalea Cotton squinted at the paperwork. "Where on earth do people come up with these names?"

Azalea—my teenage work-study assistant from the local high school—stood at the back of my van and checked to make sure we had everything we needed to paint a portrait of champion racing greyhound Bella Bailout X Three Peat Ingathered. I was assured by Jeff Abernathy before I arrived that the hound could simply be addressed as Bella—*if* I felt the need to do so.

"I think there's some kind of system or convention or something about their names because they all seem to have these crazy word salad combinations." I pulled out the bag of acrylics and piled it atop the folding utility cart. "At least we don't have to find a way to get it *into* the painting. Mr. Abernathy let me know that the name will be on a plaque attached to the frame."

"I'm surprised they don't just stuff the dog and nail it to the wall," Azalea murmured. It was an uncharacteristically dark sentiment from the ordinarily cheerful girl, and I looked at her with surprise. A faint blush reddened her cheeks. "Sorry. I'm sorry. Zach says that these greyhound tracks are nothing more than commercialized animal abuse. Racing can be dangerous, they can be injured. Heart attacks, even. I know this is a job, and you can't turn it down and all, but I just...I *don't* like this place."

"I don't know that I'm a huge fan of the greyhound racing, either, Azalea. But I *do* know that Martin does his best to demand a high level of care for the dogs while they're here."

Azalea gave me a skeptical look but didn't respond.

At least, I was *pretty* sure he did.

It was hard to know anything about Martin these days, really.

What started as a move to an Arkansas small town so I could find my birth parents had morphed into a paranormal drama I *hadn't* anticipated. I came hoping to open Mystic Moon Gallery, teach people art, sell paintings, share some coffee, and discover my origin story.

And technically, I did that—sort of.

I *didn't* expect that origin story would involve a ghost living in my building, a greyhound familiar, twenty-seven witch bottles with women trapped in them, and a super-powered vampire working for a rich guy (with mommy issues) who *also* seemed to have no problem finding loopholes to manipulate me.

The vampire, I mean. Not the rich guy. Or maybe the rich guy, too.

I could barely keep it all straight anymore.

Oh, and let's not forget a town curse and the snarky old woman that slapped me, ensuring this was all *my* problem.

Gideon, my greyhound, barked.

"What, Gideon?" I piled the last of the stuff on the cart. "You have friends here you're excited about seeing?"

My greyhound barked again and wagged his tail.

"Thank goodness *you're* out of that terrible place, Gideon," Azalea said, scratching his long head. "If only your brothers and sisters were, too. Zach says that it won't be too long before all animal exploitation is ended, you know. Then *all* greyhounds can find their forever homes, just like *you* did."

Considering how many people were getting wealthy off this track, I found it hard to believe the end of greyhound racing was imminent.

* * *

"Are you the *artist*?" a husky voice asked as we approached the dog play area. A statuesque woman dressed in black from head to toe stared me up and down as she leaned against the fence. Her hair was styled in a severe bun, and dark sunglasses hid her eyes. She was wearing the *brightest* red lipstick I'd ever seen.

"Yes, ma'am." I nodded and looked around for Jeff Abernathy. Squinting at her, I tried to recall who Bella belonged to. "Are you...um, Ella Grayson? Do I have that right?"

"Obviously," she responded with a head toss. "Do I look like I should be hanging out in animal stalls, Ms. Delphi? No. No, I do *not*. Please," the pompous woman waved away my hand as I extended it. "I don't shake hands with people. A simple verbal greeting will do, will it not?"

"Wow, what crawled up *her* butt and died?" Azalea whispered. She leaned in to take my paint back from me.

"Be nice," I whispered back, even though I agreed wholeheartedly with the girl.

In a town full of interesting characters, this woman was *definitely* toward the top of the list. She looked like she would be more comfortable sipping coffee in Paris or espresso in Milan. Instead, she was standing in the dirt, her Manolo Blahnik heels dusty.

"Can we get started, please?" Ella asked me haughtily.

I looked around but didn't see a dog. I wasn't sure how Ella Grayson expected me to get started without the subject of the portrait, but this woman struck me as someone who didn't bother with small details like that. "Sure, can you tell me a little about what you want in the portrait?"

"It's a *dog*, Ms. Delphi. Just *paint* it so I can ship it out of here," the woman spat as she examined her long blood-red nails. "I don't care what the painting looks like. I don't even care if it's any good. This portrait wasn't *my* idea, and I'm certainly not paying for it."

"I'm sorry, I'm confused," I said, frowning. "Whose idea was it, then?"

"Ours," Jeff Abernathy said as he and his son, Hoyt, walked toward us with a beautiful fawn greyhound on a lead. Gideon barked, and the dog barked back. "Since Bella won a certain number of top races, we're contractually obligated to the track to provide a portrait of the dog for the Champions' Hallway. Miss Cotton," Mr. Abernathy nodded to Azalea. "Miss Grayson."

"It's *Mrs.* Grayson," she told him arrogantly.

The elder Abernathy glared at the woman without responding.

"Um, I don't mean to tell you your business, Mr. Abernathy, but are you *sure* that's the right dog?" I stared as the two dogs jumped excitedly around each other. As Bella leaped up, I could spot a distinctly male appendage that seemed out of place on a dog named *Bella*. "That dog is male."

"I would *kindly* ask you to keep your opinions on the appropriateness of the dog's name to yourself, Ms. Delphi," Ella Grayson said with a shake of her head. "The dog was named after my recently deceased wife, Bella. She loved that dog more than *anything* in the world." The woman winced as if admitting that had been painful.

"I'm so sorry to hear about the loss of your wife," I told the hard woman. Then I frowned. "If your wife loved the dog so much, where are you shipping it off to?"

"That flea-bitten animal is worth a small fortune," the widow sneered. "I have no use for it."

A flash of anger crossed Azalea's face.

"I'm going to watch the proceedings from up

there," Ella Grayson continued, pointing toward the air-conditioned windowed suites for dog owners. "As soon as this woman is done with her doodles, Mr. Abernathy, I *expect* you'll have that dog packed up and ready to go."

"Yes, ma'am," Abernathy answered tightly.

We watched Ella Grayson walk away.

"Well, she's a piece of work, isn't she?" Hoyt asked out loud to no one in particular.

"I never understood how a nice girl like Bella Grayson could marry such a tart shrew," Jeff told his son as he glared after the woman. "I'm not particularly fond of all the lesbians we've got running around in this town, but Bella could have found a better one than *that* if she looked hard enough."

"Are they both from here?" I asked as Azalea and I set up the easel and paints. "Mystic's End, I mean."

"Bella was," Hoyt nodded. Then his forehead wrinkled. "She met Ella when she went off to New York to try and be a model or something. The Grayson family wasn't all that thrilled when Bella came back with *that* one in tow."

"Don't you tell tales about them to the likes of her, boy," Jeff Abernathy warned. He took a deep drag off his cigarette.

I turned. "I'm sorry, did you say 'the likes of me'? What does that mean?"

"Don't think we forgot what you did to poor Hoyt here. Or that trick you played on me to get that dog." Abernathy senior pointed to Gideon, a look of longing in his eyes. "One year, *two* champions lost, and you almost got my son thrown in jail."

"Your son stole money and pushed someone down a flight of stairs, Mr. Abernathy," I responded smoothly. "He got away with all of it. He wasn't questioned about any of it in the end, so I don't see what your issue is."

"You got him *all* riled up about Rowena Clutterbuck again, woman. And don't *you* sass me," the elder Abernathy warned, stepping forward menacingly. "I called you because you're literally the only commercial artist in town. Not because I forgot what you did."

"Dad, why don't you go back in and finish that transfer paperwork." Hoyt stopped scratching Bella's neck and turned to face his father. His forehead was wrinkled with concern. "Martin *told* you to be nice to her, and you're not being very gentlemanly, Pop. I can take care of this."

I sighed.

Martin Salvi, the operator of the Mystic's End Greyhound Track and Entertainment Complex, was one of the wealthiest, most powerful, and most handsome men in all of Mystic's End. He also had a crush on me, acted like we were together, and could be a gigantic pain in my keister.

"Never *could* be kind to people that threaten my family," Jeff Abernathy huffed.

"I'm just here to paint a painting, sir," I told him respectfully. "That *you* called me to paint, by the way."

"Keep your hound under control," the man barked in response. "Greyhounds are *fast*, they shouldn't be off lead *ever*. Not for one second in the open, you got that?" He looked from me to his son.

"My dog's fine, sir." A long pause ensued as the man looked at me.

"You keep an eye on that dog," Jeff barked at his son again. "She may be willing to lose *her* dog, but I ain't willing to lose that one. Our insurance premiums will go through the roof and that Ella woman will wring out every penny she can like it's water and we're a wet washrag. You got me?"

"I hear you, Pop."

* * *

Gideon ran in circles around Bella while I tried to paint her—him.

"Hoyt, let's give her—um, him a break and let

them run around a bit." I looked up at the noonday sun, squinting. "The dogs could probably use some water and time to stretch."

The big man nodded and led Bella toward a fenced-in area. Gideon quickly followed, and as soon as Bella's lead was unclipped, the two dogs took off like a shot. Their eight paws hitting the dirt sounded like a thundering herd of cattle. I assumed greyhounds couldn't jump very high since the fence was only about four feet tall.

That assumption later proved to be incorrect.

But I'm getting ahead of myself.

Azalea and I sat on a bench surrounding the small dog area. Hoyt walked over tentatively and held out icy cold bottles of water, which we accepted gratefully. When he gestured toward an open space on the bench, I invited him to sit down.

"You don't like me much, do ya?" he asked abruptly.

"You work at a greyhound track, so *I* don't," Azalea volunteered quickly.

"You killed someone and then hid it, and him, for twenty years," I added.

"I didn't *mean* to hurt Spike," Hoyt told me. "I actually kinda liked the guy, you know. Besides, he was dead, right? Not like *he* cared whether he was stuffed in a wall."

"You'd be surprised," I murmured without elaborating.

Spike *did* care. Due to Hoyt Abernathy's decision to cover up Spike's accidental death—a claim I wasn't *entirely* sure was the truth—the dead punk's soul had been trapped in the dwelling where he died for over twenty years. A place I happened to buy (not realizing it came with a punk spectral roommate).

"Love can make you do crazy things, I guess," Hoyt sighed.

Azalea hummed in agreement with grave disinterest.

"Love isn't an excuse for taking someone's life," I told him.

"It was an *accident*. I told you."

I didn't respond.

"I feel *so* bad for that dog," Azalea sighed, watching Gideon and Bella happily race around the enclosure at breakneck speed. "Just shipped off somewhere for money. It's horrible. What if he has dog friends?"

"Well, she *can't* keep him here," Hoyt said, lowering his voice. "The Graysons are coming after her with everything they got. So Ella's selling everything of value to out-of-state buyers as quickly as she can before Bella's family really gets going. I guess she's hoping they won't be able to stop her."

I turned. "What do you mean?"

"Oh, that whole thing's a mess," Hoyt shrugged. "Bella's grandpa owned oil lands in Texas, and he made a bucketful of money. *She* came into her trust at twenty-one, met that Ella woman in New York at twenty-two. Now, at twenty-four, she's dead? Suspicious as all hell, they think."

"What does the county coroner think?"

Hoyt gave me an odd look.

Right. I forgot. Bobby, the county coroner, was barely functional on a good day.

And he seemed to have very few of those.

"Scratch that. Next question. How did Bella die?"

"Undiagnosed heart condition, the Doc claimed." Hoyt rolled his eyes. "That girl was on the volleyball team, track and field. A heart condition, my left—"

I cut him off before he could name a body part. "When did Bella Grayson pass away?"

"Just a couple of weeks ago. Didn't you hear about it?"

"No. I've been kind of busy."

Busy was an understatement.

Besides running my art studio, I was also trying to learn how to scry. This was instrumental to my finding twenty-seven witch bottles hidden around Mystic's End—so said a magical book that a grove in the woods gave me. Witch bottles that contained the souls of women descended from the coven that initially founded this town.

Martin Salvi's aunt, a partial-witch originally from Mystic's End, had found three.

I had not tried to open them.

Not yet.

"Sir!" Hoyt jumped to attention. "We were just letting the dogs stretch their legs, sir." I looked up, expecting to see Jeff Abernathy coming toward us.

But I didn't.

It was Martin Salvi, Jeeves trailing him as usual.

TWO

I didn't expect to see Martin and Jeeves that morning.

But I also didn't expect to *not* see them, either.

Martin Salvi was the operations manager of this track, a place locals called "The Complex" for short. Besides the greyhound racetrack, it had restaurants, a hotel, gift shops, a casino, a performance hall, and, of course, a strip club. It was a little Las Vegas right here in Arcadia County, Arkansas—a place designed to lure tourists, get them drunk, and extract their money.

The Complex was owned by a bunch of bland sounding corporations, shell companies put in place to hide that it was owned by the mobster Martin Salvatore, aka the *Dreamboat Don*.

Martin's father.

Though few people knew that.

Just like few people knew Jeeves, Martin's body man, was a vampire.

"Martin." I nodded and got up. I winked at Jeeves. "Sparkles."

Jeeves looked back at me without changing expression—even though I *knew* my brand new nickname for the manipulative vampire got under his skin. Which didn't sparkle, despite the nickname. But he mentioned he hated the sparkle vampire books and movies (just like every other real vampire), and a way to annoy him was born as if it had fallen into my lap.

Hoyt stared at me with something akin to awe. He didn't know Jeeves was a vampire, but he—like everyone else—knew Jeeves was dangerous.

"Hoyt, Azalea, can you excuse us for a moment, please?" Martin asked in a tone that ensured they knew the question was not really a question. He extended an arm out to me, but I walked around and past him toward the edge of the field, deftly avoiding his invasion of my space.

"What's up?" I asked once they caught up with me.

"You're avoiding my aunt's calls," Martin said, a hint of accusation in his tone. "*And* mine."

"I'm not *avoiding* the calls. They come to my cell phone just fine. I'm just not returning them once I get the message," I explained. I leaned against a wooden fence post.

"Why?" Martin asked as Jeeves bristled at my flippant answer.

"Because I'm not going to break a magic bottle open and release whatever's inside until I know for sure what's in it, and what I'm freeing. And that's all the two of you want to talk about," I said politely. I tried to hop up to sit on the fence, but I slid off with an ungraceful thud. "And by the way, I thought you and I *agreed* you would back off with the possessive stuff."

"What possessive stuff have I transgressed with *now*, pray tell?" Martin asked in a silky smooth voice. In his head, I heard the echo of Jeeves's telepathic communication to him.

The Abernathy men must have said something about your directive. I warned you to tread lightly, Martin, Jeeves told him. *You need her.*

"Telling Jeff Abernathy to treat me nicely." I glanced at Jeeves, his expression unchanged.

The work I'd been doing with Miss Bessie on honing my control over my powers was clearly paying off. Though to be fair, hearing a telepathic thought *directed* to another was like a radio broadcast anyone with a decent amount of telepathic oomph could tune in to.

"My apologies if that bothered you," Martin replied so quietly I wasn't sure I heard him. His eyelids closed slightly, and his head leaned forward as if he were confessing some long-hidden secret. "I would never want to cause you any distress."

I shrugged, wondering why Martin had to turn every apology into some earth shattering, smoky-sexy confession. I'd heard it all before, and while his sexy-at-volume-10 thing used to make my heart skip a beat, the past few months had *definitely* drenched my attraction a bit. "Whatever. Just quit with the be-nice-to-Fortuna-or-else crap like I need respect because of my close association with you. I still don't like it. Probably never going to like it. Even if we wind up dating—"

He jumped in and cut me off. "Have you given some thought to—"

"Which we're *not*," I cut him off right back. "Not now, maybe not ever—but if we *were*, I wouldn't like the possessive thing, either."

Back away from her, Martin, Jeeves warned him. *She's becoming defensive.*

I turned and stared at Jeeves. I wondered if Martin had been some inept nerd until he had a vampire trailing him around, helping him with women. "And you're on notice, too. Don't think I forgot about *your* epic urn manipulation. You got me, Sparkles?"

Jeeves nodded once. *She does that just to aggravate me.*

I toyed with shooting back a comment that would make it clear I could eavesdrop on the vampire's directives to his charge, but I decided not to. I still wasn't sure whether I could trust Jeeves or Martin, and the fact that I could hear the vampire's thoughts in Martin's head could come in handy.

It was dishonest, a little.

And I hated being dishonest.

But, well...these two came up with the rules to this *hide important information* game.

All I was doing was following the rules they set up.

* * *

The dogs continued to prance and leap in the smaller enclosure while I walked back to Azalea and Hoyt. When I got closer, I could see the two were arguing.

"They *like* to run! You're out of your mind!" Hoyt told Azalea hotly.

"How can you *not* see that making dogs run in circles as fast as they can is just flat out animal abuse?" Azalea snapped back, her eyes filled with unshed tears and pink suffusing her cheeks. The seventeen-year-old stood over the bigger man, her fists balled as if she was about to hit him. "How would you like to live in a tiny box most of your life? And then when you're let out, it's like *Run, Forrest, Run!* Put yourself in their shoes—"

"Hey!" I called, walking faster. "What's going on over here?"

"She just started rambling on about how the dogs are treated terrible, and I'm like...Man, those dogs eat better than I do most days!" Hoyt said. "Her and that stupid group PeeGrrr—"

"It's *not* a stupid group!" Azalea shot back. "They work to make sure all greyhounds find forever homes, and that none of them ever have to run in circles so stupid humans can bet on which one will get to a fake rabbit the fastest! They're *wonderful* people!"

"PeeGrrr? What's PeeGrrr?" I asked in confusion. I put an arm around the angry girl. The name was like the sound someone made if they'd drunk a bunch of water while suffering from a urinary tract infection.

"PftEoGR. People for the End of Greyhound Racing," Azalea told me. "As soon as I turn eighteen, I'm going to start a chapter right here in Mystic's End, and I'm going to put an end to this torture for the dogs!" Turning back to Hoyt, she screamed, "You watch! I will!"

Azalea's mind was a jumble of images—not an uncommon thing when people are highly emotional or angry. Images of greyhound dogs unhappy and whining mixed in with pictures of the handsome Zach Johnson expounding on the perils of greyhound racing and the success Rhode Island had in closing all tracks but one.

Of *course* there was a guy involved in this meltdown.

"Azalea, we're not here to pass judgment on the track, or the people that work here," I told her sternly. She glared at me, but her diatribe against Hoyt and what he did for a living ended in sullen silence. "Hoyt, my apologies for Azalea's tantrum—"

"Tantrum!" she burst out, her eyes narrowing in anger. "The dogs—"

"Hold on," I told her, looking up. "Where are they?"

"Where are *who*?" she asked.

"The *dogs*, Azalea," I said, pointing to the fenced-in play area.

The three of us turned toward the yard and looked, but the two dogs were nowhere to be found.

"They can't jump that fence, can they?" I asked Hoyt.

"They can, but they don't. There's usually a bunch of handlers around the perimeter with leads, and they're trained to come to the lead, so...I mean, I've never seen one, but..." Hoyt scanned the area around the grounds, but no greyhounds of any color could be seen. "Oh, man, Dad's going to *kill* me."

Hoyt rushed off without talking to us, the lead dangling loosely in his hand.

"Gideon!" I yelled, booming a telepathic shout behind the call. "Gideon, get *back* here! And bring your friend! Now!"

Seconds later, the greyhound sailed over the manicured bushes from the direction of the forest. His tongue lolled out, and he was breathing heavily as if he'd been running.

"Good dog," I told him as I kneeled in front of him. Looking him in the eye, I asked, "Now, where's Bella?"

Gideon looked away from me.

"Gideon!" I snapped my fingers, and the dog looked back, his head tilted. He nosed me and then licked my face. "Where's Bella?"

Gideon looked away again.

It wasn't until this replayed a third and a fourth time I realized there wasn't some squirrel in the distance distracting Gideon. Gideon, my beloved pet and valiant familiar, was flat out *ignoring* my question.

"Azalea, Gideon came from that direction," I pointed toward the large fence. "There's a gate over there. Go look in the woods and see if you can spot Bella. Wait, here." I rummaged around in my bag and pulled out a zip lock bag full of bacon treats. "Maybe you can coax him with this."

Gideon whined as his eyes followed the bag in Azalea's hand. The further away she got, the louder the whine grew until the dog gave a plaintive wail when she—and the bacon—disappeared through the gate.

"If you wanted one, you should have brought Bella back with you," I told the hound. I looked around quickly to see if anyone could overhear, and then turned back to Gideon. "Spill it, dog. I can't afford to get sued if that greyhound disappears. Where is she? I mean he? Where did Bella go? Is Bella hurt out there?"

Gideon sneezed. An image of a happy Bella running free flashed in my mind.

"He's okay?"

A bigger, more vibrant, pulsing image of a happy Bella running free slammed me, hard.

"Okay, *okay*, I get it. But where is he?"

An image of a gray stop sign.

"I don't understand what that means, Gideon. What does a stop sign mean?"

A hazy yellow-gray image of me. And an image of a stop sign.

"Are you telling me to *mind my own business?*" I asked him incredulously. "Gideon, that dog belongs to that Ella woman. I know that you don't like to think of yourself as property and all, but dogs are property in the human world."

Gideon growled.

"It's the truth!"

An image of me talking to Martin and Jeeves. Suddenly, I heard my own voice. *And by the way, I thought you and I agreed you would back off with the possessive stuff.* Gideon looked positively smug as he stared into my eyes, his breathing shallower now that he'd rested.

"You're getting too creative for your own good, Gideon." I stood up and looked around. Azalea wasn't back, but I did spot Hoyt Abernathy running back toward me. His father, Martin, and Jeeves were not far behind him.

Great.

"If this turns into epic drama and you could have stopped it, dog, I'm not giving you any bacon for a *week.*"

* * *

THE GREYT ESCAPE 25

"What happened?" Martin asked me.

"I don't know, honestly," I said as we all continued scanning for Bella. "After you and I talked, I came back over here. Hoyt and Azalea were arguing, and I think everyone got distracted. That must have been when the dogs jumped the fence. Speaking of, why on earth would you have an off-leash area with fences that greyhounds can jump?" I asked Jeff Abernathy.

"I *told* you to keep the dogs on a lead," he snapped back without answering.

"My dog seems perfectly well-behaved without one," I answered. "Lots of dogs go off-leash."

"Not greyhounds. Greyhounds are the fastest dogs on earth, Fortuna," Martin explained. "They can go up to forty-five miles an hour. If a greyhound doesn't want to be caught, a greyhound's not going to be caught. It's generally accepted that a greyhound should be on a lead at all times for the safety of the dog and the handler's ability to keep control of it."

"Which brings me back to the short fence," I pointed.

"The fence wouldn't have mattered if you'd kept the stupid dog on its lead!" Jeff Abernathy shouted at Hoyt, and I watched Hoyt wither beneath his father's fury. "I *told* you, I don't care about *her* stupid dog! I care about Bella! Ella Grayson hasn't signed the transfer papers yet!"

Gideon growled at Mr. Abernathy ominously.

"Where's Azalea?" Martin asked.

"I sent her into the woods to look for Bella. Gideon came from that direction when I called him," I pointed. "I figured that was a good place to start since the dogs probably ran off together."

"If they ran off at *all*," Hoyt jumped in. "Dad, that girl is a member of PeeGrrr! I bet that she set this whole thing up just to take Bella!"

I held up my hand. "Now, wait a minute—"

"That's it, *I'm* calling Clutterbuck," Jeff Abernathy glared at me. "I *knew* using you was a mistake. I should have taken a photo of the stupid mutt and had someone photoshop it into a painting. If you weren't sleeping with Salvi—"

"Hey!" I said hotly. "You called *me* for this, remember? Who I'm sleeping with or not sleeping with shouldn't have anything to do with this."

"Well, if I'd known your girl was one of those PeeGrrr psychos, I never would have called you! Wouldn't have mattered what *he* said!"

"That's enough, Jeff," Martin warned. Jeeves stepped up closer to Martin and glared at Jeff. "There's no need to call the police. We can take care of this ourselves."

"My insurance ain't gonna pay for that dog

without a police report, Martin, and you *know* it. And that Bella Grayson is going to have a lawyer here as soon as she hears—"

"As soon as I hear what?" the woman in the dark glasses asked haughtily as she walked up.

Gideon growled again.

THREE

"So, a *dog* jumps over a fence, and you rush right over, but a guy keels over dead after being electrocuted, and you're good? People slammed in the head with a rock, no big deal. A runaway greyhound, though, and you're Johnny-on-the-spot?" I asked Chief Clutterbuck. "Does a dog that jumped a fence and went for a run really demand the attention of the Chief of Police? Seriously?"

The chief's eyes glittered with annoyance while we stood together against the fence, his bushy eyebrows arched. "Ms. Delphi, can you just *answer* the question? Did you *know* that your assistant was a member of a terrorist group when you brought her here?"

"A *terrorist* group?" I asked, shocked. Even for Chief Clutterbuck, the claim was a dangerous stretch. "Look, Chief, the girl's been dating Zach Johnson. Sure, he came back from college with an animal activism hobby. She got interested in it, too, yes. But Azalea Cotton is not some radical animal rights activist that throws paint on people walking down the street. She's a seventeen-year-old girl. She's *not* a terrorist. She'd never hurt a fly."

It was half an hour since my assistant Azalea had disappeared behind the fence, and she still hadn't returned. Chief Clutterbuck and Detective Beau Conroe were questioning everyone. However, their questions seemed to imply a certain number of assumptions.

"Call June Johnson right away," he told Beau. "I want her to bring Zach into the station."

"You got it, boss," Conroe nodded. The serious-looking detective was already pulling his phone from his slacks' pocket. "Should I tell her what this is about? Have a car go pick them up?"

"Have you *met* June Johnson?" Clutterbuck asked.

"No, sir."

"That woman's so contrary, she floats upstream, *and* her boy stays in the shadow of his Mama's apron. You don't wanna spook her, or they won't come in. You just keep in mind she's got money enough to lawyer up right quick, and treat 'em accordingly."

Detective Conroe nodded again, then turned to walk away. I turned back to find the chief standing with his arms crossed over his chest, eying me with suspicion.

"Disappointed I didn't bring your pet detective, Ms. Delphi?" Clutterbuck asked.

"*Excuse* me?"

He glanced toward Martin and Jeeves as if to make sure they were far enough away not to hear his next comment. The two were talking to an angry Ella Grayson. A frustrated Jeff Abernathy stood nearby. Hoyt sat slightly behind his father, looking glum.

Once the chief was certain no one could overhear, he leaned in so far I could smell the onion bagel he had for breakfast on his breath. "If I find out you had something to do with this, Ms. Delphi, I'm going to get an immense amount of pleasure seeing your tight little hippie ass thrown in jail. And your *boy* won't be able to save you this time."

His statement was so vulgar, I was *genuinely* shocked. Too shocked to speak. Clutterbuck and I were never on the best of terms, and he was as corrupt as anyone else in Mystic's End—but he'd never expressed so much naked hostility toward me before.

Gideon growled and projected the image of his teeth sinking into the Chief's flesh.

I won't say what flesh.

But I could tell it was pornographic despite the dog vision haze.

We need to go over there now, I heard Jeeves's think at Martin. *Clutterbuck just said something to Fortuna I suspect could lead to him being turned into a frog during their conversation.*

Clutterbuck *didn't* know that Jeeves, being a vampire, had *exceptional* hearing. From what I'd read, it was possible he could have been on the other side of the track and still picked out our conversation if he tried hard enough.

Frustratingly, I could not hear Martin's response. Whatever magic his mobbed-up witches had wrapped around him protected his thoughts from me.

For now, anyway.

"How are we doing over here?" Martin asked pleasantly—and maneuvering so he was standing directly next to me facing the chief. Jeeves planted himself slightly behind me on the other side.

Good to see that the possessiveness lecture I gave was heard.

"Ms. Delphi and I were just discussing her

assistant," the chief told Martin as concern replaced the sneer that had taken up permanent residence on his face. "I think it's *clear* what happened here. Ms. Cotton intended to steal the dog. I suspect she's meeting with one of her co-conspirators in the woods right now to hand him off."

"That's absolute crap, Clutterbuck!" I fumed. I felt two hands lightly rest on either arm, but I ignored Martin and Jeeves. "You've done exactly zero investigation about any of this. You're passing judgment on Azalea because of some preconceived notion you have about her views on greyhound racing!" Shaking off the hands and pulling myself to my full height, I finished with a warning. "If you rush to judgment and harm that girl in any way, I will *not* let this stand!" I shouted.

"What are you going to do, Ms. Delphi?" Chief Clutterbuck asked with an amused tone.

"I—"

"Are you planning to arrest the girl, Chief?" Martin pulled me in next to him, hard, and squeezed my arm with enough force I felt its warning.

Before I could turn on him, Gideon pressed against my leg, and I felt the hot fury at Clutterbuck and Martin drain away rapidly.

"If you are," Martin told him, "I just want to

make it clear that she's represented by counsel. No one should question her."

The chief stared at Martin, calculations of risk visibly dancing in his eyes. Clutterbuck glanced down at me and then back up to Martin.

Then he shrugged.

"Then I suggest *you* find her and tell her. Because if *we* find her first, we have no obligation to let her know that. You're not an attorney."

Chief Clutterbuck spun on his heel and walked away.

* * *

"You *can't* stay out of trouble for a *minute*, can you?" Martin asked me. I pulled my cell phone from my pocket and tried to call Azalea. I waved him away when I heard her phone ringing from the direction of the picnic table.

"Her *phone's* here," I told him, pulling it out. "If she was meeting someone to hand off a dog, she would have her *cell phone* with her."

"Unless they had a prearranged location to exchange the dog," Jeeves pointed out.

Reaching forward, I grabbed Jeeves's shirt collar and jerked him toward me so I could stare him in the eyes. "Whose side are you on, Sparkles?" Jeeves stared back, a slight smile on his face. As if my anger, and the danger Azalea was in, was amusing. It just infuriated me more.

Sorry, Martin, I heard Jeeves say. *I can follow the girl's scent once Fortuna leaves. And we still have to calm Ella Grayson down.*

My eyes narrowed. Why not tell me he can track her? Why did Jeeves have to wait until I left?

"Ella!" a voice screeched from the greyhound building. "Ella, baby, what happened? Why are the police here?"

A tipsy Evangeline Laroux, wine bottle loosely held in each hand, hobbled toward the severe woman. She tottered on six-inch high heels, and the five of us stared as if waiting for the drunken stumble and fall that *looked* inevitable. Despite a few close calls, the buxom platinum blonde closed the distance between her and Ella and draped one arm around her target.

"You're drunk. It's as if you were squeezed out of a bartender's rag," Ella frowned, eyeing the glamorous Evangeline.

"Y'all say that like it's a *bad* thing," Evangeline giggled.

Ella sniffed the air and shrugged the drunk woman off of her. "You smell like you want to be left alone, dear." She shoved, hard, and Evangeline stumbled toward a bench and landed with a plop, one bottle breaking. The area suddenly smelled like expensive red wine.

"Oh, Ella!" Angie snorted, slapping her thigh so hard she yelped. Then she laughed again. "You're so funny! Oh, Martin!" the drunk woman breathed. "You're here! You can come and help me up, baby doll." She held her arms out wide, a dreamy look on her face.

Hoyt watched the scene with a sad look on his face.

"Help her," Martin told Jeeves quietly. For a moment, Martin looked surprised, and a look of what *might* have been pity crossed his face. In a flash, it disappeared just as quickly, leaving him looking mildly annoyed.

"You s-s-stay away!" she slurred as soon as Jeeves stepped one foot toward her. Ella rolled her eyes.

"Leave her," the hard woman said, yanking Evangeline up from the bench she had pushed her into. "I'll get her back to the Centre Club myself. I can deposit her with Jack on my way out of this miserable place."

"You're such a goof ffriend," Evangeline mumbled.

"Thank goodness her father didn't see her like this," Ella told Jeeves, referencing Chief Clutterbuck's departure right before his daughter

Evangeline Laroux (previously Rowena Clutterbuck) spilled onto the scene. And I do mean *spill*—her ample chest was perilously close to exploding out the top of her skintight dress. "Her father would have lectured her for an hour seeing her in this state." Ella's face scrunched again as Evangeline belched.

"Does her father not see her at all?" I mumbled surprised. I don't think, in all the months I'd lived in this town, I'd ever seen Evangeline Laroux sober. Not once. "I mean, this is *pretty* much that woman's steady-state, isn't it?"

Neither Jeeves or Martin responded.

"Did you get it done, Ella?" Evangeline asked her friend and then hiccuped. "Did you wreak your Bella havoc? Bella Havoc. Oh, I like that," Angie grinned, laughing. "That would be a *great* stage name, wouldn't it. Bella Havoc. Bellahavoc bellahavoc bellahavoc," she slurred, and then laughed uproariously. "It makes my tongue feel funny. Bella Havoc, star of the stage and—"

Suddenly, Evangeline Laroux lurched, threw herself against the wooden fence post, and vomited forcefully into the bushes. It happened so fast I didn't have time to jump into Ella Grayson's head to see what the havoc Angie spoke of called up in the severe woman's mind.

* * *

"What was that about?" I asked Martin once Ella dragged Evangeline Laroux toward the track's entrance. Hoyt followed them a respectful distance behind, watching his ex-girlfriend. As far as I could tell, he hadn't said a word since she stumbled out into the yard.

"Which *what* are you asking about, specifically?"

"The Bella havoc stuff she was referencing," I asked him.

"The name she chanted?" Martin asked, confused.

"No, the *havoc* she referenced. Selling a dog someone else wants doesn't seem to me to be an act of widespread destruction. What was she talking about?" And was she talking about the dog, or the recently deceased Bella Grayson?"

"Well, there's no dog to sell right now, so I'm not sure it matters."

"The chief of police showed up here to investigate a dog jumping over a fence, and before even finding said dog, he decided to arrest my assistant for dog-napping?"

"No, for theft," Jeeves said. "Dogs are property in this state."

"I *know* dogs are property in this state." I threw

my supplies back in the boxes and bags I had brought. "Why does everyone feel the need to remind me dogs are property in this state?"

Gideon shoved an image at me of Azalea walking away.

"I know, buddy, we're going to go look for her," I promised the concerned hound, putting away the last of my stuff. "We'll just put all this back in the van, and you and I will go look for Azalea in those woods back there."

Jeeves and Martin shared a glance.

I know it wouldn't be safe for her, Jeeves replied to something Martin thought but I couldn't hear. *I can't track the dog and follow Fortuna simultaneously. You need to let me know what you want me to do.*

"Is there anything back there," I pointed, "that I should know about? Construction or caves or anything that might make the terrain dangerous? Those places are *probably* the first place I should check, too. The cops may not be concerned since they solved the case and all, but I'm worried that Azalea or Bella—or both—might have gotten hurt."

"Jeeves will go with you," Martin said, nodding toward the gate. "He can track the dog or Azalea by scent, at least for the next few hours. Unless you have some magic?"

I shook my head no. "Still a neophyte, pretty

much. Though I can repair anything here that needs repairing." I heaved the bags onto the cart and pushed it toward the parking lot, but Jeeves gently took it from me and moved on ahead.

"Did you mean what you said?" I asked Martin. "About the lawyer?"

"I tend to agree with you. It's unlikely Azalea is some terrorist mastermind. I don't know that I have your same confidence she didn't do something illegal because she felt it would benefit the dog," Martin confided as we walked slowly. "I'll give Gerard a call and have one of the attorneys in his office notify the courts and police formally that she has representation."

"I don't know if she can afford—"

"We'll work that out later," he said, cutting me off. "Let's just worry about finding them both safe and sound."

Usually, I would have turned Martin down in a heartbeat and given him a stern lecture about how awesomely independent I was. But I didn't know what Azalea's financial situation was. After hearing Chief Clutterbuck's plans to arrest Azalea for a crime, one he didn't even know for sure had happened? I didn't feel comfortable turning down Martin's offer on her behalf.

"Thanks," I told him. "I appreciate it."

"That's what friends do, isn't it?" he asked me.

"Help each other out when they can. If I have something you need, it's yours."

I swallowed.

It may have remained unsaid, but the expected quid pro quo was clear.

FOUR

"Do you still have the stone?" Jeeves helped me step over an unsteady pile of rocks. We were picking our way through dense heaps of fallen oak and pine trees in an undeveloped area owned, but not used, by the track. The branches above blanketed us in dark shadows. Through their cooling canopy, I could see golden light peeking through.

"What stone?" I asked, slapping at a mosquito.

"You know what stone," Jeeves responded.

Well, of course, *I* knew what stone.

I just didn't think *he* knew what stone.

Soon after realizing that Jeeves was a vampire, I contacted Charlotte for advice. Samson, her snarky black cat (that could, when the mood struck him, transmute into a gigantic panther god) tossed me a black stone through the rainbow cauldron mist. As long as I kept it against my skin, the cat assured me, the vampire could not read my mind.

I *hadn't* told Jeeves how I blocked him out, though.

That he seemed to know the shield protecting me was generated by a tiny gemstone stuck in my bra didn't thrill me. I, admittedly, hadn't been super-careful when Jeeves wasn't around. Reluctantly, I realized I would have to change that. Showering in a bikini, maybe? I cringed at the thought of sleeping in a bra.

We hiked through the woods without talking. How long? I couldn't tell you. I heard the sounds of running water, the whispering of the trees as they gently swayed in the wind. I heard Gideon sniffing, and the vampire breathing in sharply sometimes. As if he was tasting the air.

But I never heard footsteps, and no one ever called out for help. After an hour, I grew frustrated.

"There are *acres* of this place; there's no way we're going to find Azalea out here," I complained. I sat down and pulled out some bottled water. "And the dog could be miles away by now. This is a pretty easy hike, though. Maybe she tripped over a fallen tree and hurt her ankle. The elevation changes are slow-rolling, though. Not a lot of rocks," I mused out loud and then took a swig. "It looks so easy to get lost back here."

"How so?" Jeeves asked.

I looked around. "Everything looks the same. Every tree looks like *every* other tree. There's no path." I looked behind us and then swiveled my head to look toward an area we had not explored. "I remember we came from that way, but only because of the way I'm sitting. If you spun me around a few times? I'd be lost."

"I'm surprised that you would say that." Jeeves sat down on a stump across from me and gestured up toward the trees. "I look around, and it seems like each individual tree has a spirit. Even if they look alike physically, they appear quite different from one another to me." He looked at me curiously. "A moment ago, I would have assumed you and I both could see that difference. Strange that you don't."

"Why would you assume that?"

"We're both paranormal," he answered.

"Did someone teach you how to do that?" My brows rose.

"Of course. I got extensive training."

"Well, I *didn't*," I told him. I stood up and packed away the half-full bottle of water. "I got turned into a witch because the Witches' Council decided that I, as a partial-witch, had no right to live. It was the only way Charlotte could save me. Though, to tell you the truth? Even if it wasn't under threat of death, I probably would have done it anyway."

"Did your maker—"

"My what now?"

"Your *maker*," Jeeves repeated. "The one who turned you witch. Did she teach you about the things you needed to know?"

"Charlotte didn't *turn* me. She and Gunther's father had to do it together. From what I understand, witches don't go around *making* witches. It's a genetic thing, not a magical thing. At least, not usually a magical thing," I shrugged. "The ringmasters were something different."

"Yes, I know of the circuses," Jeeves nodded. "My people were quite amazed at the idea of a traveling power. They always wanted to check one out, but the protection that surrounded the circuses barred vampires."

Before I could answer, a shriek pierced the silence of the clearing. Jeeves leaped to his feet, and the two of us ran toward the sound.

* * *

An involuntary shudder ran through me as I stared.

"So, that's...unexpected." Jeeves stared at the hole in the ground.

It was square-ish, almost like a shaft. A ladder stuck out of the top, leaning against a reinforced wall before descending into the darkness below.

I leaned over and peered down. With no light, I couldn't tell how deep it went, or what I would find if I descended beneath the earth.

Which I hadn't decided to do.

"I sense nothing," Jeeves said finally. "You?"

I shook my head, no. "I don't think anybody's down there. But something made that noise, right?"

"Maybe it was just the wind. As for that? It could just be someone's personal crystal mine." He also leaned forward and stared down. "It goes down about twenty feet."

"You can see in the dark?"

"I wouldn't be much of a vampire if I couldn't."

I swung my leg over and placed my right foot on a rung just below the surface.

A steady hand reached out and grabbed my shoulder. "What do you think you're doing?" Jeeves asked incredulously. "You don't know what's down there, whether the shaft is stable."

"I also don't know if Azalea's down there unconscious, and that's why I can't sense her," I told him, dropping down a rung.

The vampire's grip got tighter.

"I smell no human, Fortuna," Jeeves assured me. Then he sniffed the air again, his eyes unfocused. "Well, I smell no human in the immediate vicinity. Someone has been here within the past day or two. And not Azalea. The girl has a distinctly youthful scent. This smell is not female, and it is older."

"You can tell *all that* by sniffing the air?" I asked him without climbing back up.

"I can, on occasion, pick up someone's scent months after they have been in an area."

"You're like a bloodhound. Damn," I told Jeeves, impressed. "I wish I'd known that when I was chasing that stupid urn theft all over town. Oh, wait, right—that was *you* manipulating me." I stuck my tongue out at him and dropped another rung on the ladder. "So, you wouldn't have been much help."

"I have all manner of manipulations at my disposal," he told me calmly, tugging upward lightly on my shoulder. "When I need to, I *do* use them. For example, if you move one more rung down on that ladder, I *will* pluck you off it and carry you back to the track to ensure you don't get hurt. Granted, it's a straightforward manipulation, but I promise it's quite effective."

"What happened to the whole *witches can kill*

vampires so I have to respect you thing?" I asked him without moving.

"Have you *learned* how to kill a vampire?" Jeeves asked with an amused twinkle in his tense eyes. "You have a habit of delaying things that have to do with magic, so I suppose I'm gambling my immortality on the likelihood you have procrastinated. As usual."

"That's a *hell* of a gamble," I said with menace.

"No disrespect meant, but I don't believe it is," Jeeves answered with a smile. The vampire looked amused. "Now, will you agree to come back up, or will this pleasant walk in the woods become confrontational? I'd prefer the former, but I am *quite* prepared for the latter."

I wanted to argue with him, but he was right.

I *hadn't* bothered to learn.

I wasn't really *avoiding* it anymore like I used to. I wasn't having some big, emotional struggle about magic and Mystic's End or anything. What used to be a dodging of truths I didn't want to deal with was now just plain old procrastination.

That, and it never occurred to me that Jeeves would *hurt* me.

For some inexplicable reason, I trusted him.

In fact, I trusted *him* more than Martin Salvi—even though there was no *real* reason I should. I had lots of reasons not to trust either of them. The vampire also warned me that if I tried to hurt Martin, it was likely that I *wouldn't* be able to trust him.

"If Azalea had gotten hurt down there and she was bleeding, you could smell it?"

Jeeves's eyes softened, and his grip relaxed a tiny bit. "I promise you, Fortuna, your assistant is not lying at the bottom of that shaft bleeding. If she was, I would go down there and get her myself. I'm just concerned about your safety, and I don't believe there is anything regarding the dog Bella or Azalea down there."

"Well, what *do* you think is down there?" I asked him as he helped me climb back up.

"Your guess is as good as mine," Jeeves answered.

He suddenly avoided my eyes.

"Right, back to the track, then." I snapped for Gideon, and he came running.

As we walked back, Jeeves's expression indicated he may have been communicating telepathically with Martin, but I heard nothing. It answered one question about my ability to overhear Jeeves's directives to his boss.

I wasn't slipping past Jeeves's defenses.

I *was* slipping past Martin's.

* * *

"Did you know about this?" I gasped at Jeeves. Without waiting for an answer, I ran toward the scene. "What *the hell* are you two doing?" I shouted.

Azalea, covered in dirt that highlighted her streaking tears, was being placed roughly into the back of a police car by Detective Beau Conroe. The car's strobe lights pulsed into my eyes.

"Ms. Delphi, do you *really* need the situation explained to you?" Chief Clutterbuck asked as his daughter, Evangeline Laroux, hung unsteadily off his arm like he was about to escort her to a dance. "Do the handcuffs and police cruiser not convey enough information to you?"

"So, you found Bella?" I asked him.

Clutterbuck stared back.

"We didn't need to find the dog," Beau Conroe told me, closing the back door on Azalea. "She was gone long enough to have passed it on to one of her animal terrorist friends. She didn't come back for an hour. She's posted countless times on the town Bulletin Board that all the dogs should be set free, that this place should be closed down. Enough for me."

I glanced through the window. Azalea looked tiny on the large bench seat, her body shaking with fear. "What *evidence* do you have? None of that was *evidence* of anything."

"I'm not going to play this game with you," Detective Conroe told me with a shake of his head. "I've seen you twist Gabe up into a pretzel with your feminine wiles, and I'm not letting you do it to me, you hear? This case is practically open and shut."

I looked down at my jeans, t-shirt, and sneakers caked with mud. An odd streak of paint appeared here and there.

Feminine wiles?

"Azalea has a lawyer," I told the detective. He slid into the driver's seat and shut the door, so I raised my voice. "You can't question her without a lawyer present, Detective!" He didn't acknowledge my words. I banged on the window before anyone could stop me. "Detective, are you *listening* to me?"

"Ms. Delphi, there's room enough for *you* in that back seat," Conroe snapped at me after he cracked the window. "If we uncover that you were part of the plot, we'll be back for you, too."

"That's enough, Detective Conroe," Jeeves warned, stepping close beside me.

"Fortuna, can you call my mom?" Azalea asked. Her voice was small, quiet, and choked with terror. "I'm so sorry, Fortuna, I didn't mean—"

"Stop talking, Azalea," I cut her off. "You say nothing, nothing at all, without a lawyer. Do you hear me?"

Her eyes widened, and she nodded vigorously.

"You shut her up to protect her, or you?" Beau Conroe asked me.

"She *has* a lawyer," I told him again one last time.

"Like *that* matters," he chuckled. Rolling up the window, he winked at me and pulled away. The siren wailed, and he raced off at twice the speed limit—as if he carried a long-sought serial killer.

"I don't *believe* this," I muttered.

"Fortuna, let's find Martin," Jeeves suggested quietly.

"Yes, run along and find one of the men you seem to have wrapped around your finger, Ms. Delphi," Chief Clutterbuck cracked. "Is it Jeeves today, then? No?" I stared at the Chief angrily. "Martin? Or perhaps you'll run to Gabe and see if *he* can explain what's going on. Are there any more I'm leaving out? You seem to have built up quite the collection."

How had a man like this *ever* been hired on to be Chief of Police? And what happened that his hostility had gone from implied to *right* the hell out in the open?

I noticed, not for the first time that my aversion to cursing was fading away the longer I lived in Mystic's End.

"Daddy, Martin's *mine*, remember?"

Evangeline purred and snuggled in her father's arm.

"Of *course* I remember, kitten," Clutterbuck told his distinctly un-kittenish daughter in a syrupy-sweet voice. "I think Mr. Salvi's spell is being broken, don't you? After all, it was Martin that called me to let me know that Azalea was here and could be picked up."

"He did *what*?" I asked sharply.

"Martin Salvi let me know we could come to arrest the peeg."

I frowned. "What's a *peeg*?"

"A member of PeeGrrr, young lady. We in law enforcement call them peegs."

That seemed ironic in ways I didn't feel like pointing out.

Under the circumstances.

"Isn't that right, Mr. Salvi?" Chief Clutterbuck gazed past me.

I turned to find Martin standing behind me.

He stared back.

And said nothing.

FIVE

"Why would he *do* that?" Pepper asked when I stormed into my shop. She pulled the phone away from her ear as I hung up the other end of the phone call.

"Because it's more important for him to keep his cozy relationship with Clutterbuck, clearly." I threw down my purse and marched behind the counter. I glanced at the day's schedule, frowning. "I have two classes this afternoon. Damn it, I hate having to keep *canceling* on these people."

Silence. "Whoa."

I looked up. "Whoa? What's whoa?"

"You said *damn it*. Casually," Pepper pointed out, a worried look on her face. "Like it was just part of your vocabulary."

"So?"

"So, you don't *do* that. You're the girl with a stick up her butt about all manner of cursing." Pepper squinted at me. "Hell, Fortuna, you bitch at me when I say curse words that are in the actual bible."

"Don't get some idea you can start truck-driver level cursing all over my shop," I warned her. Leaning down, I lugged out the heavy, leather-bound book an isolated grove had presented me with and tried to tug it open. I didn't know that the book would do anything different than it usually did—refuse to open if I was without Miss Bessie—but I'd been repeatedly told I didn't turn to magic enough in a crisis.

Okay, magic. Here's your chance. Open up and tell me what to do. I'm listening.

I reached out and gently, so gently, placed my finger beneath the archaic-looking cover. Hoping against hope the darn thing would just open, I pressed upward.

Nothing.

Locked closed as if it had been welded shut.

"Oh, come on! Enough with this, will you?" I exploded, shouting directly at the book. "I don't want to drag Bessie over here every time I want to check you to see if there's anything useful! You want me to be all *super-magic witch bottle breaker extraordinaire?* Fine. Help me out here!"

The book trembled in response.

"Whoa. Did you *see* that?" Pepper scrambled to stand across from me and stared down at the tome. "You saw that, right?"

I nodded.

"What do you think it means?" Pepper whispered as if she was afraid the book would overhear her. "Was it a ghost? Do you see anyone here?"

I shook my head, no.

"Maybe you should try and open it again," Pepper suggested warily.

Then she stepped back to ensure a safe distance between her and whatever the book might do to us because I screamed at it. I stared at her.

"What?" she asked tartly.

I rolled my eyes and looked down.

Before I could touch the book, its heavy cover flew open as if a high wind had whipped through the shop. The front page, which *had* contained a directive to learn how to scry (which I, um, hadn't done one inch beyond what I already knew), had *new* words scrawled on the parchment as if written in calligrapher's ink.

· · ·

S TOP BEING SNIPPY

"R emarkably helpful," I grumbled, slamming the cover shut.

"Well, they let you open it by yourself, at least," Pepper pointed out with a hopeful lilt to her voice. "That's progress, right?"

The cover whooshed open again.

T HE WITCH HUNTERS HAVE YOUR FLOWER. IS THIS REALLY THE BEST USE OF YOUR TIME?

"M y *flower*?" I frowned.

"Azalea. Her name, it's a flower," Pepper said, tilting her head. "Huh. The witch hunters. That's an *interesting* thing to call the police."

"I still don't trust this book," I said, closing the cover again. "I don't know who's behind it, who's sending those messages—"

"I thought Miss Bessie said it was the trapped witches?"

"Lots of people *say* things," I shrugged. "I don't

know. Look, I love Bessie, and I trust that she *believes* what she's telling me. But it's all just old stories, right? Who's to say if it's true? Whatever's sending those messages, the book is right about one thing. It's clearly not going to help me with Azalea."

"So, I have to ask. Did you *really* think it would?" Her tone wasn't contemptuous, but it definitely crept up toward cynical.

"I continue to maintain hope that there's a positive to all this garbage," I told her, and shoved the blank paged volume back beneath the counter. "So far, not so much. Okay, so, let's talk plans. Let me know if you think this is a good idea."

Pepper and I spent the next half hour planning out our next steps.

* * *

"I'm surprised you showed up," I said as Gabe walked in and took his place at the back table of my empty business. For a second, I wondered if we should meet in the *muse room*. I could *use* a little bit of wind-chime and incense calm of late.

"Yeah, well, Chief Clutterbuck *specifically* ordered me not to get involved with the case, or to share any information with you, and then I saw Ollie slip out the back," Gabe admitted. He hitched up his chair. "Ollie," he nodded to his best friend, already seated at the table. "Pepper," Gabe greeted his ex-girlfriend. "Given the trouble the three of you tend to get into, I figured I needed to head on over and check out what y'all got yourselves into."

"The *three* of us?" Ollie asked, laughing. "When did *I* get looped into this as a permanent member?"

"You're here, aren't you?"

Ollie laughed again. "Point taken."

Pepper stared at Gabe a while. "Fortuna's *cursing*. Gabe's doing the exact *opposite* of what he's ordered to do. And the book is opening on its own without Miss Bessie—getting a little ornery to boot. Is it backwards day and someone forgot to tell me?"

"What book?" Gabe asked, confused.

"One thing at a time," I told him, staring *hard* at Pepper. "Book's not important."

"Oops," she said, and then shrugged. "My bad. Nothing. It's just an art comic book."

Gabe knew a lot—he knew I was a witch, for one. But he knew nothing about Miss Bessie, the curse of the town or the mystic of Mystic's End. He didn't realize that the witches of the Delphi Coven had been trapped in witch bottles and hidden around the town.

Or that one of them could be his mother.

Or that I'd been charged with freeing them.

"Okay, so explain what happened this morning," Gabe said, running a hand through his short hair. "I know the dog was Bella Grayson's, and it now belongs to Ella, her wife."

"Oh, *jeez*," Pepper's face puckered as if she just sucked on a sour lemon. "You didn't tell me this involved the Grayson clan's craziness. This just got *stupidly* complicated, and we haven't even really started yet." Pepper leaned down to her backpack and unloaded stacks of notebooks onto the table.

"Wait a minute, what do *you* know about it?" Gabe demanded, his eyes widening with each pad Pepper slapped onto the table.

"I mentioned some weirdness to Pepper a couple of weeks ago. You know, when Bella came through the coroner's office?" Ollie sat up straighter. "I picked up her body from the hospital, and everything was all normal-like. Seems like just a fluke, you know? Happens sometimes, and an undiagnosed heart condition isn't *that* uncommon, you know?"

"But something didn't look right?" Gabe asked, frowning.

"She was young, so we had to do postmortem toxicology along with the autopsy. I sent it off, and I saw it when it came back—if *I* was running that case? I would have listed the cause of death as a fatal drug overdose. The free morphine concentration in her blood was through the roof, and she wasn't given any pain reliever at the hospital. I checked," Ollie admitted. "She was wheeled in flat-lining."

"Was she a known drug user?" I asked.

"No. Which made me a little suspicious, so I tested her hair."

"Her *hair?*" I asked, confused.

"Hair testing can detect drug concentrations over time," Gabe explained without taking his eyes off Ollie. "Were there any?"

"No, nothing. Bella Grayson's hair was as clean as a whistle." Ollie sighed and reached into his jacket pocket to pull out a piece of gum. "I *did* bring it to Bobby"—the county coroner—"but he didn't want to hear it. Said that the Graysons were good people that didn't need this kind of scandal on top of Bella being gay and all. That she technically died when her heart stopped, and no one needed to know what contributed. And then he threw both reports away."

"Ugh, this town," Pepper complained. "Equating being gay with *dying* from an opioid. That's ridiculous."

"Who was the detective assigned to the case?" I asked Gabe.

"Natural death." He shrugged. "At least as far

as what Ollie's office had to say about it. Don't see why *anyone* would be assigned to it."

"You think this was just Bobby doing a favor for a prominent family?" I asked Ollie.

"All Bobby seems to *do* is favors for prominent families," Ollie admitted. He shifted in his chair toward me. "Some months it seems like that's the only reason he has the job at all, truth be told. Hoping the town elite will open up the doors of the private supper clubs at the track to him if he just does *one* more thing for one more person. Never happens," Ollie chuckled. "Doesn't stop him from trying."

"Okay, so, weird. But what does it have to do with the greyhound?" I asked. Gideon perked up and wagged his tail at the mention of Bella (the dog). "Don't you *even* wag your tail at me. I know good and well that you know more than you're saying."

Gideon's tail drooped.

"So, once Ollie told me about all that weirdness, I started digging into the probate stuff," Pepper said, her breath accelerating with excitement as she shuffled through papers. "Ella's going to get one *hell* of a payout—millions, in fact—from a life insurance policy. She gets the house, the art in the house. That's where this all started to get hostile, I think."

"The art?"

"The family has a bunch of paintings done by Reginald Grayson—they're descendants of the guy. He's some famous painter or something."

"I know who he is." I nodded. "He was almost as famous as John Trumbull."

Three blank faces stared back at me.

"John Trumbull? The painter?" I asked again. The faces remained blank. "Trumbull's painting *Declaration of Independence* is one of four paintings hanging in the United States Capitol Rotunda? You've probably seen it dozens of times in school textbooks?" Still blank. "You *have* heard of the United States Capitol, right?"

"Yes. Sorry that we're not well-versed in art, Professor Smarty-pants," Gabe said.

"Anyway, Grayson's paintings are a lot like Trumbull's. They, along with some others, basically painted the American Revolution. Their paintings are worth tons of money."

"And old Reggie's priceless paintings were *not* supposed to be in the house when Bella died," Pepper said. "See, the weird part of the will? It didn't name art or pieces that went to Ella. It just did this blanket *the house and all its contents* thing. Bella's parents were having their house refurbished, and so the family's *whole* art collection was in Bella's house temporarily."

"That seems *incredibly* suspicious." I frowned.

"That, and the fact that Bella's parents had just left for Paris for a few weeks? You bet. They just arrived back yesterday." Pepper pulled out an itinerary.

"Yesterday?" I asked, surprised. "Their daughter *died* almost two weeks ago!"

"They were on some kind of religious retreat where they couldn't be contacted," Pepper explained. She pulled out another stack of papers and shoved them toward me. "The family lawyers have been doing what they can, trying to contest what they have the power to contest, but without the Graysons' signatures? It wasn't easy."

"From what I heard, Ella's been selling things for cash as fast as she can get it out the door," Ollie added. "Including that dog."

"Okay, so, what we have here is...a mess," I sighed.

"What we need to decide first is what we're focusing on," Gabe said, his face concerned. "A young girl is in jail. That started out being our highest priority. Is it still?"

"Yes." I answered.

"Okay, then that's the angle we go at it," Gabe nodded. "Why don't you take us through what happened this morning, step by step?"

I nodded and began my tale.

* * *

"Jeez, I thought this was complicated *before*," Pepper muttered while she frantically took notes.

"I don't think Azalea had anything to do with the dog being kidnapped. I mean, *if* he was. Not directly, anyway," I explained as I finished. "But she's got stars in her eyes for that boy, Zach Johnson, and I don't know much about him. He's perfectly polite when he drops by here, but there was always something a little off about him. If you know what I mean."

"He *can* be as demanding and arrogant as his mother," Pepper nodded.

"My worry is that he used Azalea to kidnap the dog. I mean, *if* that's what happened. And again, I'm not at *all* saying that's what happened. Considering all the Grayson drama?" I held up my hands. "I don't know what to think anymore."

"He's never been in trouble with the law *here*," Gabe scanned through the information he had pulled up on his tablet. "But he *does* have a couple of charges pending in Rhode Island. Blocking a road. Breaking a glass window at a pet store." Gabe's eyes widened, and then he squinted. "Stealing a truck full of...hamsters? I *think* that's what it says."

"That sounds all animal-rights-like to me," Ollie told Gabe.

"But the Graysons came back into town yesterday," I interjected. "It could have just as easily been one of them coming to snatch Bella's dog back. Everyone told me this morning how much Bella Grayson loved that greyhound. Maybe they were appalled at the thought Ella would sell it?"

"And there's a third possibility. The dog just got loose and ran," Pepper said.

"Aren't they microchipped?" Ollie asked.

"Yeah, but it's not a tracker," Gabe told him. "If we scan it, we'll know it's the right dog, but we can't use the thing to find out where the dog is now. We have to have the dog already. Very short range."

"You sure you don't want to chime in here?" I asked Gideon, who watched the table's discussions intently. Everyone turned to look at my greyhound. "Something you want to share? Something you want to tell us?"

Gideon sneezed.

What good was a magic greyhound familiar, anyway?

An image of Bella Grayson's will flashed in my mind. The words FREE were painted across them in bold red.

"Yes, Gideon, you *have* free will. You know what you *don't* have?" I asked him.

The dog's ears perked up.

"Free bacon. You *need* me for that. So, I'll ask again. Anything you want to tell us?"

Gideon whined.

"I would *swear* that dog can understand you," Gabe murmured.

"Oh, he understands me, all right," I told Gabe.

Gideon barked.

SIX

A reluctant Gabe Wilcox followed me up the steps to Azalea's house. "Are you *sure* this is a good idea?" he asked me.

"You've never been a teenage girl, have you?" I reached out and rang the doorbell. A cheerful chime echoed inside the small house. A dog barked, and a young boy yelled for his mother. "Even if Azalea doesn't *confide* in her mom? My bet is Mrs. Cotton has lots to say about the relationship between Azalea and Zach." A loud crash echoed from inside, and the boy's calls were joined by a second voice almost indistinguishable from the first.

Seconds later, the door flew open, and a frazzled woman in a bathrobe and curlers greeted us. "Fortuna! What on *earth* happened this morning? Why would the police arrest Azalea?" she asked frantically, waving us in. "I can't get the police department to tell me anything!" Noticing Gabe, her face grew angry. "*Why* would you arrest my daughter? She's a *good* girl!"

I held up my hand. "Detective Wilcox isn't here officially, Mrs. Cotton—"

"Call me Amelia," Amelia Cotton said, waving to a couch covered with toys. "Just push all that stuff onto the floor. And then be careful not to trip on it."

"Amelia, have you met Zach Johnson?" I asked as I sat down.

"Of course. He and Azalea have been dating a few months." Her eyes narrowed. "What does he have to do with this?"

"Maybe nothing. The police think that Azalea is a member of PeeGrrr, an animal rights group that wants to end greyhound racing. They suspect that Azalea, or Zach—or the two of them working together—*might* have kidnapped Bella and Ella Grayson's greyhound. *That's* why they arrested her."

"That's *ridiculous*," Amelia protested, kicking plastic toys out from around her slippered feet. "Sure, Zach and Azalea are both involved with that group. They even took me to one of their meetings. This isn't some militant group wanting to tear the

track down brick by brick, though, Fortuna. It's a
bunch of old ladies and mothers of young kids. I
think Azalea and Zach are the youngest two in the
group!"

"Did you know that Zach Johnson had charges
pending in Rhode Island?" Gabe asked her.

Her face fell, and she looked troubled.
"Charges? As in *criminal* charges? Zach Johnson?
Are you sure?" Gabe nodded. "No. Azalea never
told me that he'd been in trouble with the law.
What did he—what was he accused of doing?"

"It *sounded* like protest-related activities," Gabe
told her. "But he *was* accused of breaking a window
at a pet store. When protests upgrade to violence
and vandalism, that tends to indicate a certain level
of willingness to go *against* the law to achieve an
end. Do you think Azalea shares his feelings or has
that same willingness to go outside the law for her
beliefs?"

Amelia chewed her lower lip and then sighed.
"To tell you the truth, Detective, I just don't know.
If this was just some political stand, I would say
that she wouldn't—she's a *good* girl, and she knows
right from wrong. But these are living, sentient
creatures that she cares about a great deal. If she
thought she was helping that dog, saving it from
suffering?" Amelia wrung her hands nervously. "I
just don't know. Right and wrong can get

confusing when something you care for is truly suffering."

I cringed that Amelia, in her worry, had just admitted to a detective that her daughter *might* be capable of orchestrating the theft of the greyhound. Glancing over at Gabe, I noticed he didn't have a recorder out, and he wasn't taking any notes.

"I wanted to stop by and let you know that Martin has provided a lawyer for Azalea—"

Amelia immediately cut me off. "Martin Salvi? The *head* of the greyhound track?" she asked, her tone shocked. "Why on earth would he do *that*?"

"Probably to impress Fortuna," Gabe interjected. I glared at him. "Martin's been trying to woo her since she came to Mystic's End."

"I *can't* afford an attorney that charges what one of his attorneys would charge!" Amelia said. The seven-year-old twins, Alder and Anthony, peeked around the corner from the dining room to watch us. "My husband's on a business trip about to make a *huge* purchase of balled and container-grown trees for fall tree planting season!" she informed me, referencing the Cotton Nursery she and her husband, Todd, owned. "We *won't* see that money back until early next year!"

"I'll take care of it," I told Amelia quickly. I felt a little dishonest saying it. I knew Martin was unlikely to allow me to pay for the legal services—

but I didn't know how to explain why the head of the greyhound track was so generous to a suspected greyhound thief. "Azalea was working for me when this all happened. I'll take care of the legal bills."

Amelia stared at me, tears in her eyes. "But I...I can't let you..."

"You can." I left no room in my tone for an argument.

"But...What if she did what they *said* she did?" Amelia whispered. "What will happen to her?"

I didn't have an answer.

* * *

"That seemed like a waste of time," Gabe said as we got back into his SUV.

"She was worried," I told him. "Checking in on someone going through a bad time is *never* a waste, Detective. Besides, I wanted to make sure that Amelia knew we were looking into things, and about the lawyer. Azalea *is* a kid. It was only right. Speaking of...why weren't you taking notes or recording that interview?"

"I'm not working on the case," he said as we pulled out of the subdivision and onto the main road. "I told you, I was ordered to stay away from it."

"And me. I heard you."

"So, no notes to take. Did you use your voodoo on her to see if she was hiding something?"

I turned and stared at him. "My *voodoo?*"

"Whatever you call it. Your psychic thing."

"No, I didn't," I told him.

"Why not?"

"Because she's Azalea's mother. That, and I didn't get the sense that she was hiding anything from me. It's not something I just do willy nilly."

"So, wait." Gabe turned right toward the Graysons'. "You could sense that she wasn't hiding anything, but you didn't use your psychic powers on her? Wouldn't you sensing that *be* a psychic thing?"

"There are different levels. Think of it like a swimming pool. Just being in the vicinity, I can see that there's water—can tell certain things like color. I can smell chlorine. It's *there*, so the fact that someone's around me means I can pick up on certain general things. More if I look *directly* at the pool. Or the person. If you get my meaning."

"Like whether someone is hiding something."

"Right," I nodded. "If I want to know more, I *can* dip my toe in. I'll get a little more information. But it's my *choice* to dip my toe in, and I can choose not to. Block it out if I don't want the information."

"Or you can choose to plunge right in if you want to know everything."

"Yes," I admitted. "*Or* someone can be

splashing around so violently that the water from the pool comes out and drenches me whether I want it to or not."

Gabe frowned. "I'm not sure I get your meaning."

"People can project mentally, or emotionally, without *realizing* they're doing it. They can psychically scream the same way a person can vocally scream. Or they can be so emotional they're just spraying and telegraphing their thoughts *all* over the place. Getting hit with that *can* take me by surprise, or happen so fast that I have trouble blocking it out."

"So, why would you block it out? Isn't more information better?" Gabe asked.

"It can be uncomfortable seeing inside people's heads," I admitted. "For example, I knew you were attracted to me the first night we met."

"You did, did you?"

"I did."

"Why didn't you say anything?"

I laughed. "What was I supposed to say? I know that you suspect I'm a hippie gypsy come to fleece the town, but you clearly think I'm cute, so let's get coffee?"

"Would you have?" he asked in a smooth drawl.

"Would I have what?"

"Asked me out for coffee?"

I didn't answer.

"Sorry," Gabe said after a too-long pause. "I didn't mean to make you uncomfortable."

"You didn't. Well, not in the way you think," I told him after another too-long pause. "To tell you the truth, I don't know. I don't know that I want a relationship right now with anyone."

"Could have fooled me," he responded a little too quickly.

"The thing with Martin's...changed. In weird ways. Ways I didn't expect. We're *not* dating. And honestly, with everything that's happened, I don't know that we'll ever date now."

"What happened?"

And there it was again.

Gabe knew things, but *not* everything. Not the important stuff. Not the most important things going on in this town, at least as far as magic and curses and imprisoned spirits were concerned. He had always fallen back into his job's ethics—ethics he seemed to take seriously even if no one else in the town did. Even if it inadvertently made him part of the problem.

So long as Gabe took the side of Mystic's End, I didn't know that *any* of us could tell him what was happening.

"Every time you go quiet, Delphi, I get the

sense there's a whole lot you're not telling me. And I'm not psychic *or* a witch like you."

I sighed. "We're all just trying to keep you from feeling torn between your job and...and..."

"The truth?" he asked with a glance and a lopsided grin.

"You can't handle the truth!" I joked with a terrible Jack Nicholson impression.

"I can," Gabe told me once he stopped laughing. "I'm *here*, aren't I?"

"You are here," I admitted. "And *we* are here. I think that's the house."

"This conversation isn't over," Gabe told me, chuckling.

I smiled faintly as we pulled in the driveway of a smaller home than I expected—considering the reports of the Graysons' wealth.

* * *

"I'm sorry. You're an *art* teacher?" Darrell Grayson looked back and forth between Gabe and me. His wife, Joanna, stood beside him, her face red. She clutched a white, embroidered handkerchief in her hand.

"I was painting your daughter's dog this morning at the greyhound track—"

At the mention of Bella Grayson, Joanna wailed.

"Now, now, Mother, none of that," the gruff Mr. Grayson patted his wife's shoulder. His eyes swept over the two of us standing on his front porch. "Do you see what you've done? Haven't we been through enough the past several days? You're here about a *dog*?"

"My apologies, Mr. Grayson. My name's Detective—"

"You're a *detective*?" The older man's eyes widened. "Well, why didn't you say so, son! Come *in*, come in!" Mr. Grayson reached out and pumped Gabe's hand, practically yanking him through the archway. "The police told us all this was a civil matter and not to bother them! What changed your mind?"

I followed the couple into a sitting area off the main foyer. How did the parents of a dead citizen get blown off by Mystic's End Police Department at the same time the *chief* raced to a greyhound track about a runaway dog?

Gabe pulled out his notepad and skimmed over an unmarked, clean sheet. "Mr. And Mrs. Grayson, let me first say how sorry I am for your loss. Now, the dispatcher didn't give me too much information about why you called us," Gabe lied more deftly than

I *ever* would have believed he could. Though I guess, technically, it wasn't *really* a lie. There was a police dispatcher. That dispatcher hadn't given him much —or any—information. "Why don't you tell me, in your own words, what you believe the situation is?"

"That woman killed our daughter!" Joanna Grayson burst out, tears flowing.

"What woman?"

"Ella! That Ella woman!"

"And why do you believe that to be the case, ma'am?"

"Just look at what happened. Look!" the woman said, a hitch in her voice. "Ella gives us a two-week spiritual retreat in Paris *as a gift* where we're completely unable to be contacted. Just *one day* after we're in isolation, our precious daughter Bella dies unexpectedly. We *could* be contacted for emergencies, but no one did! Ella didn't *bother* to get a message to us before she started selling off the family heirlooms!"

"Was it just the two of you at the retreat?" I asked.

"And our son, Brock," Mr. Grayson said as Joanna cried into his shoulder. "Brock is...was Bella's twin brother. At the retreat, Brock seemed to *sense* something was wrong. If only we'd listened to him," Bella's father said sadly. "Though by the time he said something, our beautiful Bella was already gone."

"Is he here?" Gabe asked.

"No," Mr. Grayson answered sharply.

"Bella is dead because of her. She *killed* our Bella, I *know* it," Joanna said viciously. "But you people said she just died of a heart attack! Natural causes! Our Bella was as fit as a fiddle! It's just not *possible!*"

I noted that Bella's parents were given the false cause of death and seemed unaware of the powerful opiates in their daughter's system. Had they been, they would likely be at the police station throwing rocks through the windows in fury, judging by their anger level.

"Did you have an issue with Bella's wife, Ella?" Gabe asked.

"That *viper?*" Joanna hissed. "Of course we did. We *always* did."

"She was not the type of woman we would have *ever* thought our sweet Bella would wind up with," Mr. Grayson told us. "I always thought Bella would wind up with that quiet Claire girl she met playing softball. They were such an *adorable* couple."

"Do you remember Claire's last name?" I asked him.

"Of course. Claire Chaplin. Lovely girl."

I did my best not to drop my jaw. I was *friends*

with Claire. Miss Bessie's caretaker was so quiet, and she'd never mentioned an ex-girlfriend. Then again, she and I weren't *that* close, and Claire tended to be kind of private.

"It doesn't seem like either of you had a particular problem with Bella being gay." Gabe frantically wrote notes down in his notebook.

Joanna stopped crying and stared at him, hard. "Are you implying that we *should* have, Detective?"

"No, ma'am," he answered quickly. "Just trying to get a clear picture of the situation."

"Is *that* why the police aren't investigating our daughter's death, son?" Mr. Grayson asked, a hard edge to his voice. "Because my daughter was married to a woman, her life's end isn't worth—"

"Absolutely *not*, Mr. Grayson, and I profusely apologize if my question implied anything like that," Gabe said, meeting both of their gazes. "Unfortunately, they're just questions I have to ask."

"They are *not*." Joanna's tone made clear how hurtful she found the implication. "They are not questions you have to ask. Someday, perhaps, you'll see that."

"Well, ma'am, perhaps someday *all* parents will make sure that I *don't* have to ask that," Gabe told her, his eyes soft. Joanna looked as if she wanted to say something more, but she nodded sadly and dabbed her eyes. "Again, my apologies if the question upset you."

"Is there anything we should know about the legal goings-on?" I asked them.

"Didn't you say you were an *art teacher*?" Mr. Grayson asked me suspiciously.

"Sorry, Mr. Grayson." Gabe reached out and lightly placed his palm on my arm. "She's correct, though. If any civil legal maneuvers going on could shed some light on this situation, it would be beneficial for me to know about them."

"Call Barbara Townsend," Mr. Grayson said, pulling out a business card from his wallet and handing it to Gabe. "I'll call ahead and ask her to speak openly to you about everything that's been going on. We want to help the police in any way we can."

Gabe nodded and stood up.

"Again, we're *very* sorry for your loss. Please let me know if there's anything I can do to help." Gabe handed Mr. Grayson his card, and the two men shook.

"Find out who killed my daughter, Detective Wilcox," Joanna whispered as we left. "Please. Please find out who killed my baby."

Gabe nodded once again, and then we left.

SEVEN

"Did that house look newly refurbished to you?" I asked Gabe as we drove toward the Mystic Memories Senior Living Center to meet with Claire. "I didn't see anything that looked particularly new, I didn't smell any fresh paint. You?"

"Now that you mention it, no." Gabe turned the SUV at the stoplight and slowly climbed the hill toward *Wrinkle City*, the nickname for the Mystic's End retirement home. "Who said they left because the house was being refurbished?"

"Pepper."

"Have you heard from Pepper?"

I looked at my phone. "No texts. Let me ping her." I texted her to see if she and Ollie had discovered anything more, when the car lurched to a stop so hard the seatbelt dug into my skin. "What the heck, Gabe?"

"You all right?" Gabe looked at me with concern.

"I'm fine, but what—" My sentence stopped as I looked up and found Jeeves standing in the center of the driveway as if he'd been waiting for us. "What the *heck*?"

"He's not staring at *me*," the detective grumbled. "Dude's lucky I didn't run him over. That deer catcher on the front of my truck can catch more than just deer." Gabe angrily waved him out of the way, and Jeeves stepped toward the passenger side. The vampire moved casually—as if he had nowhere to go and no place to be, and everything was happening according to plan.

Gabe pulled the car forward, and I rolled down my window. "*Why* did you do that?"

"I need to speak to you," Jeeves responded.

"So? Speak." I leaned on the open window.

His eyes moved slowly over Gabe's face. "Alone."

"Anything you can say in front of Fortuna, you can say in front of me," Gabe told him.

Before Gabe opened his mouth, I'd been willing to have the conversation in front of him. *After* he opened his mouth, however, I had a change of heart about the whole thing.

I turned and raised an eyebrow at Gabe. "Is *that* so?"

He shifted uncomfortably. "You don't want me to hear something he has to say?"

"Tell you what, why don't *you* tell me why I shouldn't be entitled to *any* privacy, and we'll go from there. Maybe I'll learn something." I waited for a response as Jeeves watched the exchange with interest.

Finally, Gabe threw the SUV into park and pulled up the brake. "I'll be inside visiting my grandmother when you're done," he countered without answering. With a scowl, he gestured for me to exit the vehicle.

"I swear, you men are such babies," I told him getting out of the truck. "This will only take a minute. I'll find you as soon as I'm done. Try and get over yourself between now and then."

"Really, I'm fine with it." Gabe forced a smile as I closed the door.

"You sound it," I called back through the open window. The scowl returned. Gabe released the parking brake roughly and pulled toward the parking lot.

* * *

"That man has feelings for you," Jeeves observed. We walked toward a large shade tree.

"Everyone has feelings for me in this town, Sparkles," I shot back. "I seem to provoke all kinds of feelings in people."

"That's not what I mean, and you know it." Jeeves looked at me with a cautious glance. "In any case, your love life is not why I sought you out. First, I want to let you know that Martin has bailed out Azalea Cotton. She's home with her mother under house arrest."

"Thank goodness. Well, sort of," I said with relief. "The house arrest thing sucks, but it's better than jail." Jeeves looked at me, an expectant air around him. Which was fair. "Look, I know things have been tense between Martin and me since the whole *lying to me about why he's here* thing, but I do appreciate it. I know Azalea didn't do this."

Jeeves eyed me skeptically. "How?"

"Because I know Azalea," I responded so definitively I *almost* believed it.

I wasn't as confident as I pretended to be. So far, there wasn't any evidence that the greyhound had been stolen, much less that Azalea had a hand in his disappearance. And the more we checked into all this stuff, the more things seemed...weird.

But none of that meant Clutterbuck was wrong in his assumptions.

Most things we were turning up had more to do with the possible murder of Bella Grayson than the disappearance of Bella the greyhound. Those two situations *might* be separate. Then again, they might not be.

"Fortuna? Did you hear me?"

"Sorry, sorry. I was just thinking," I said, my eyes refocusing.

"I said I went back to the shaft that we found in the woods with Martin," Jeeves repeated. "He could not, however, see the hole directly in front of him."

Now *I* was the one eying *him* skeptically. "What do you mean? It was *right* there. How could he *not* see it?"

"To Martin the clearing was a clearing like any other. I even asked him to reach down and try and place his hand *into* the space. He could not. To him, it was solid ground."

A hole in the ground, a ladder shaft, that only paranormals could see?

"Have you ever heard of such a thing?" Jeeves asked me.

"Sort of? The circus used to be able to hide from humans, so I guess so," I told Jeeves while nodding slowly. "I thought that was circus power, though, not run-of-the-mill magic." I studied Jeeves.

"Wait a minute. Why are you asking *me* this? Don't you guys have, like, a gaggle of mob witches on staff or something?"

A delivery truck rumbled up the hill toward the old folks' home, and Jeeves glanced distrustfully at it. Once it passed by, he turned. "I wanted to ask you instead."

"Yeah, I see that. But why?"

Jeeves turned away and looked off in the distance toward the home. His face was as smooth and unreadable (as it usually was), but the corner of his eyes pinched with tension. After a long pause, he answered. "We don't have any witches on staff here in Mystic's End, that's all."

Except for Martin's aunt.

Who lives in Martin's house.

They had a communications cauldron in a hidden room on the second floor, too. They could call any witch they wanted or transport any paranormal they needed.

Jeeves's answer didn't make sense.

Or it was a lie.

"Come on, Sparkles, what's going on?" I asked him. "Why not just ask Aunt Addie?"

"It must be frustrating for you that you cannot read me like you can everyone else." Jeeves leaned back against the tree, the pinched tension in his face gone. "I admit it's remarkably frustrating for me."

"You're playing games with me. Don't change the subject."

"This is definitely *not* a game, Fortuna." Jeeves stood up straight and met my eyes. "I take my responsibility to protect Martin very seriously. And I will protect him from anyone that tries to harm him." He paused. "Anyone. I've told you that before."

I couldn't tell whether Sparkles meant that as a threat or a confession. But there was something in the timbre of his voice, something in the *way* he said what he said. He was concerned about something. What?

I didn't know.

"Gabriel is getting frustrated," Jeeves jerked his head toward the home. "I estimate he's about two minutes from coming out here and getting you."

"Do they teach you to speak all cryptic and mysterious in vampire school?"

Jeeves laughed. "I think we evolve to this, truthfully." He shrugged. "Our predator nature affecting the way that we speak, perhaps. I'm told it's sexy in certain situations."

"Not in this one."

"I'd like to ask you to return to the woods with me to examine that shaft," Jeeves said as I turned to walk away, finally getting to the point. "I can sense what's down there to a certain extent, but I *would* feel more comfortable being accompanied by a witch. Considering."

"I can't drop everything to crawl down a ladder to nowhere. I have to find out what happened to the greyhound and get Azalea out of the trouble she's in. That's not even mentioning it looks like something weird happened with Bella Grayson, too."

"Weird?"

"Maybe murderous is a better word."

Jeeves nodded. "Would my assistance make this go faster?"

I eyed the vampire and thought about his offer.

His powers were formidable. Not only could he read people telepathically—without the same moral and ethical dilemmas I wrestled with—the vampire could affect their emotional states, so they felt more comfortable and relaxed. Jeeves was also physically strong, incredibly fast. I'm sure there were other powers he had I wasn't even aware of.

But...I didn't trust him.

"Who's guarding Martin if you're running around with me?" I asked him.

"I am." He opened his mouth, and his fangs snapped down with a click. They were long and terrifyingly sharp. Jeeves's passive expression suddenly looked menacing with the addition of two bladed weapons glinting from his open mouth. "I told you once, I can sense Martin over greater distances than you would think."

"You can't get there faster than a bullet," I pointed out.

"Martin will be fine."

I folded my arms across my chest. "You know I don't trust you, right?"

Jeeves's fangs disappeared with another click, and he smiled. "You know I don't trust you, either. I don't see what that has to do with anything."

* * *

Gabe smiled as I walked into Miss Bessie's private room, and then frowned when he spotted Jeeves behind me. Claire sat in one of the chairs by the window and the old woman leaned back in a rocking chair.

"Fortuna," Claire smiled. She looked tense, her small hand nervously running over her close-cropped hair as if checking whether it had grown enough to tug on. The small woman's eyes widened as Jeeves stepped to the side of the room and observed the group gathered.

"Sorry I'm late," I told her. I sat down in the empty chair across from her. I glared at Gabe and Jeeves. "Can you two sit down somewhere? This isn't an interrogation."

"I'm not sitting on my grandmother's bed," Gabe told me.

"Whaddya think happens on that bed, boy?" Miss Bessie snapped at him. "I wiped your butt when you were a baby with this very hand; you can sit down on my bed. You look like a pair of towering inquisitors."

Blushing hotly, Gabe sat.

"If you'll excuse me a moment, I'll get a chair from the hallway." Jeeves quietly left the room.

"What did I miss?" I asked.

"Claire was just telling me a bit about Bella Grayson," Gabe began. Jeeves brought in a chair and sat down on the far side of the room.

"We weren't together very long," Claire admitted. Her voice was timid. "Well, I guess when you consider how young we were, a year *is* a long time. It can feel like forever. I was older than she was, so to me...Anyway," she looked down. "We were together a year."

"You'd heard she passed?"

Claire nodded. "I went to the funeral. Well, *funeral* probably isn't even the word for it, really. Ella had Bella cremated within just a few days of her death. I only heard about it because of Rick Taylor, the nurse here? One of the folks here passed away, and the family couldn't get the cremation time that they wanted because Ella was insistent."

Her eyes teared up. "So, he mentioned it to me. There wasn't even a funeral announced, but I...I wanted to be there for her."

"For Ella?" I asked.

Claire's usually gentle face twisted into a mix of pain and anger. "*No.* Seeing her was probably the thing I was *least* looking forward to. Though I didn't even have to worry about it in the end," she said, sadness clouding her face. "Ella didn't attend *her own* wife's funeral, such as it was."

I nodded. "Did you and Bella still talk to one another?"

Claire turned scarlet, and I sensed shame pouring off my friend.

Suddenly, I knew.

"You were still in love with her, weren't you?"

"I didn't do anything or say anything, Fortuna, to encourage Bella to leave Ella, I swear I didn't. I would never *do* that." Claire covered her eyes with her hands and took a deep breath to calm herself. "But we started talking again a few months ago, and she was just so *unhappy* in her marriage, and..." Fresh tears ran down her face.

"Was Bella planning on leaving Ella Grayson?"

"I don't know for sure, honestly," Claire said as her eyes swam with tears. "I don't know how *anyone* could stay in a marriage that was that unhappy, so I *think* she was. Or would have.

Eventually. Bella was very old-fashioned in her way, you know? She didn't believe in divorce. So she tried." Claire wiped the tears from her face. "But we...I didn't want her to leave her *wife* for me, you know? That's just so...so tawdry and wrong. I wanted her to make the decision for herself—if she wound up making it at all. And so some things we made sure we didn't talk about."

"What was it that made her so unhappy, child?" Miss Bessie asked.

"It became apparent to Bella that Ella was only interested in money, not her," Claire told the old woman. "Ella was constantly complaining that Bella wouldn't buy her things, that their house was too small, that they didn't go on trips. I mean, the Graysons *have* money, sure. But they don't act like they do, you know? They don't buy fancy things or live in fancy ways. They like a simple life, and they donate a lot of their money to charities. Ella *hated* that. The more Bella tried to convince her to live without luxury, the angrier and meaner Ella got."

"Did Bella have any health problems that you know about?"

"No," Claire shook her head no, surprised. "Why?"

"Did it seem suspicious to you that such a young woman would die so suddenly?" Gabe asked.

Claire avoided his gaze. After a few moments, she nodded.

"Why didn't you say anything?"

"What was I going to say?" Claire shrugged, looking up at him. "The coroner said it was natural, her wife seemed not to care. Her parents couldn't be reached. Besides, what did it matter if she sold everything off and took all the money?" She clenched her fists and whispered, "Bella's *gone*. It won't bring her back."

"What about justice for Bella?" Gabe asked her gently.

"Have you *met* her brother, Brock?" Claire asked him. He shook his head no. "You should. Maybe then you'll see why *I'm* not worried about justice. Ella might want to be, though."

EIGHT

"You're awfully quiet," Gabe said as we—we being the *three* of us, vampire included— headed back to the Cotton house in the police SUV. I wanted to talk to Azalea about what happened earlier this morning now that she was out of police custody, but I wasn't thinking about that.

I was thinking about the dark shaft in the middle of the forest—a shaft hidden by magic.

"Just thinking," I told him. "Lots to think about."

"Like?"

I didn't respond. I couldn't tell him.

Or could I?

No, I couldn't. Miss Bessie hadn't told him anything yet.

But still...I mean, the magical, hidden shaft had nothing to do with Miss Bessie being the mystic of Mystic's End once. It had nothing to do with the witch bottles hidden all over the town imprisoning women that dared to question. It had nothing to do with Gabe's mother drowning so many years ago. Couldn't I tell him while keeping all *that* hidden?

"Hey, are you all right?" Gabe asked after glancing in the rearview mirror. "You look awfully pale."

"I'm fine. Just hungry," Jeeves responded.

"We can stop for lunch at the diner after we talk to Azalea."

"Unfortunately, if you'll recall, I'm on a special diet," Jeeves reminded him. "There's nothing on the menu that I can eat."

That might be the understatement of the year.

"Oh, right," Gabe said, suddenly remembering Jeeves was actually a vampire. I noticed his discomfort with the reminder immediately. "I... right. Right."

"When you and Fortuna stop for lunch, I'll run back to Grigio Hills. I'm sure Addy has prepared something for me."

Or someone, I thought to myself.

"Here we are." Gabe pulled in to the driveway and slid the SUV into park. His expression seemed troubled. "Actually," he said as the engine idled, "I think maybe I should skip this. She *is* a suspect, she's been arrested, and I *am* a detective. If she says something incriminating, I'm going to be obligated to turn it over."

"It *does* make one wonder why you're engaged in any of this at all," Jeeves observed.

"It makes 'one' wonder, does it?" Gabe asked with a raised brow.

"My apologies, Detective," Jeeves responded. "It makes *me* wonder why you're engaged in this. One's experiences shape one's expectations, and you are confounding my own at the moment."

"What's all this *one* nonsense?" Gabe snapped back.

Jeeves stared back silently.

"While this grammar discussion is fascinating, we're beginning to attract attention," I said, pointing toward the neighbors peering out their windows at the police SUV. "Why don't you drop us off here and go catch up with Pepper and Ollie? Let them know what we've learned so far and see what they have. We'll meet back at my shop at"—I looked at my phone—"three. Then we can head over to the lawyer's office."

"How will you two get back to town?" Gabe asked.

"I can call one of the cars," Jeeves told him.

"There, you see? Jeeves can call one of the

cars," I told him as I opened the door. "Oh, and one more thing. Can you find Brock Grayson?"

"He was probably back at the house with his parents," Gabe pointed out.

"He wasn't," Jeeves and I said simultaneously.

Gabe twisted around to look at Jeeves, and then back at me.

"And y'all know that how?" he asked.

"Witch." I lifted my shoulder in a half shrug.

"Vampire." Jeeves smiled.

"I live in crazy town," Gabe muttered. He motioned for us to get out.

* * *

"Fortuna, I'm so sorry!" Azalea said as Amelia showed us into the living room. The young woman was sitting on the sofa in a ball, arms wrapped around her legs. She fidgeted with a thick black cuff on her ankle. I could see a red light flashing.

Zach Johnson sat next to the terrified girl, his arm around her shoulder. He glared at us as we entered.

"Sorry for what, Azalea?" I asked gently. I made my way to a recliner next to them. Jeeves stood behind me as he always stood behind Martin—

quiet, alert, and menacing. "Did you do something you need to apologize for?"

"Don't say *anything*," Zach said with a shake of his head. "I know she's your boss, but she's dating the head of the greyhound track. That's his guard,"—Zach pointed angrily at Jeeves—"right there! For all you know, she's a part of this *whole trap*! They entrapped you just to tear down PeeGrrr! They probably have the dog themselves!"

"I'm sorry, did you say *I'm* part of laying a trap *for Azalea*?" I asked, gobsmacked at the accusation coming from the handsome young man. "Are you crazy? I'd never even heard of PeeGrrr before this morning!"

"Zach, please," Azalea said, turning toward her angry boyfriend. "Fortuna would never have done that. Why, it was her and Martin that got the lawyer that—"

"You used a lawyer that the *greyhound track* sent for you?" As he faced the tiny, shaking Azalea, the young man's face churned with fury. I could feel the energy of his anger building. He looked at her with disgust. "Azalea, are you a *complete* idiot?"

"Hey!" I snapped, standing up. "Back off, Romeo. *Don't* talk to her like that!"

"Why don't you just *get out*? No one wants you here, you *traitor*!"

"Zachary Johnson, this is *my* home," Amelia stormed back in from the adjacent kitchen. "I realize you're upset, but you will not talk to Ms. Delphi *or* my daughter in this manner, do you hear me?"

"You should calm down," Jeeves told Zach quietly, his voice soothing.

Zach's face softened as he turned to look at the vampire. I could see, and feel, the young man's struggle to maintain the fury that had infused him just moments before.

But he couldn't.

It drained out of him like air from a leaky balloon.

And he was baffled by it.

"Now, you should sit, Mr. Johnson."

Slowly, as if confused, Zach Johnson sat back on the couch. His arm lifted, cautiously, again around Azalea's shoulders.

"Hey," Amelia called sharply to Jeeves, her eyes wide.

"Ma'am?"

"Will that work on the twins?" Amelia pointed to her seven-year-old twin boys back in the kitchen. As I leaned forward, I could see they were happily drawing pictures on each other's faces—with permanent markers. "I'd pay you. Free flowers from the nursery. Whatever you want."

"Why don't you go take care of them, Amelia?"

I told her. "I think Jeeves can make sure this is under control."

"Clearly," Amelia said, looking him up and down. Then she sighed and turned. "Boys, *quit* drawing all over each other!" Azalea's mother stomped back toward the kitchen. "Your father should be home later today, and I don't want you to look like you ran wild while he was gone! This family's dealing with enough problems as it is!"

The boys laughed and ran toward the back of the house, markers at the ready.

"Azalea, what were you apologizing for?" I asked my art assistant again when the chaotic sound of seven-year-olds faded.

Her eyes jumped toward Zach and then back. "I'm just sorry that I got you in trouble is all, Fortuna," she told me, her voice shaky.

Azalea was clearly nervous about speaking in front of her hot-headed boyfriend, and I didn't know how far Jeeves's *calm-the-heck-down* power went. Or how long it lasted. I'd have to be careful with my questions.

I sat down again. "You didn't get me in trouble. I'm not the one that got arrested. But I need to know, Azalea," I said, scooting my chair closer to her. "*Do* you know where Bella the greyhound is? Is he all right? If you know, I mean. I'm *not* asking you if you did anything."

Not yet, anyway.

"No, Fortuna," Azalea shook her head. "Everything happened just the way you saw it happen," she said, glancing at Zach again, her face full of apprehension. He looked disinterested—and a little stoned. "Bella ran outside the gate, and I went after him to bring him back. When I came back, the police arrested me. That's it."

"Did anyone know we were going today?" I asked, glancing at Zach.

"Well, sure," she nodded. "I told my mom, and I told Zach."

"Do *you* have anything you want to tell us?" Jeeves asked Zach in a comforting, friendly tone.

"Yeah," he said.

"And what would that be?"

"You're traitors and animal abusers." Zach struggled to sneer. "And I'm going to put your boss out of business."

* * *

"Can't you make him confess?" I asked Jeeves as we slid into one of the track's many courtesy limousines kept on hand for high rollers. We sat across from each other.

"No," Jeeves said, pushing the button to raise the privacy partition. "I can affect their emotions, their comfort level, but I can't *make* anyone do anything they wouldn't do ordinarily. Though that *would* be useful for operational expediency," he mused. "Besides, we don't know that he has anything to confess. I sensed nothing but his anger."

"Guy that treats people like that? He has something to confess. Maybe not *this*, but something." I felt *my* anger rising as I thought back to Zach's arrogant, angry outburst. "Azalea's such a sweet girl. How could she be with such a jerk?"

I saw a flicker of something in Jeeves's eyes. "What?"

He half-smiled and responded, "Nothing."

"Come on, Sparkles, spit it out."

He glanced toward the window and back to me. Gabe was right—his face was *incredibly* pale. "I find that women often get involved with men like that. I think there is something in the female condition that confuses aggression for protection, perhaps."

I stared at him. "An expert on women, are you?"

His lips curved into the barest hint of a smile, and his eyes darkened. "I'm an expert on many things. Women, unfortunately, are not one of those things." He smiled. "How have we come to this place, you and I? Sitting in the back of a limousine discussing women."

"We're not discussing women. We're filling in the silence, that's all."

"You're feeling friendlier toward me," he said with a chuckle.

"I thought you couldn't read me." My hand immediately made for the stone in my bra to assure myself it was still in place. It was. His eyes followed my hand and then quickly moved back up to my eyes.

Damn it.

Was this whole conversation designed to get more information about how I was blocking him?

And did I just show my hand?

Or boob, as the case may be.

Go ahead, Sparkles, try and grab a handful, I thought.

We'll see whether a witch can break the arm of a vampire *real* quick.

"I said I wasn't an expert on women, Fortuna. I didn't say I was naive." Jeeves turned to the side and grabbed a glass from the center console. Placing two cubes in it, he poured some sparkling water and handed it across to me. "Here. No reason we should both be thirsty."

"Thanks," I took the glass and sipped. "Is that why you're pale? You're thirsty?"

He nodded.

"For blood."

He nodded again.

"Human blood."

"Why does it bother you so much?" Jeeves asked me, his head tilted.

"That you drink blood?"

"That's not what bothers you. I already told you that I don't have to kill. It bothers you that I'm a vampire, and I serve Martin. Your feelings for him seemed to change right after you found out what I am and how I came to work for him. In fact," he leaned forward, "you seem to be friendlier toward me than *him* of late. Setting aside the *Sparkles* nickname, of course. Which you know I can't stand."

"You don't *work* for him, though, do you?" I pointed out. "You're a paranormal slave. One of many, I might add." Jeeves was right. When I discovered Martin's mafia family had a gaggle of witches and vampires "on staff"(enslaved) to serve them, I was appalled.

"We're back to that again, are we?" Jeeves folded his arms. "When you get a viewpoint locked in your mind, you're unshakable, do you know that? How is what I am to Martin any different than what Gideon is to you?"

I blinked. "Are you comparing yourself to a *dog*?"

"Are you *truly* going to tell me you think of Gideon as nothing more than a pet? The animal is clearly your familiar."

I snorted. "And you're Martin's familiar?"

"The relationships are not *entirely* dissimilar. Why do you feel they are?" Jeeves pressed. "Why are *you* comfortable with having Gideon serve you, assuming that he will serve you, but not with my serving Martin?"

I rolled my eyes. "Sparkles, if you knew how much of my bed that dog took up and how much I spend in bacon, you'd have a better understanding of who serves who here."

The limo lurched to a stop, and I glanced out the window at Martin's mansion. I hadn't been back since the night that everything between us broke wide open, and a nervous knot formed in my stomach upon seeing it.

The driver opened the door, and Jeeves and I both leaned forward to exit. Since we were sitting across from each other, this resulted in a collision. The two of us tumbled to the floor.

I landed on my back, the vampire on top of me.

He breathed in sharply, his eyes unfocused. He stared down at me with his lips gently parted.

Holy smokes.

We stared at one another, my breath caught somewhere in my ribcage. I wasn't sure, as we stared into one another's eyes, whether Jeeves would bite me or kiss me. It felt like hours passed—

even though it couldn't have been longer than a few seconds.

"My apologies," he stammered. He pushed himself away from me and scrambled out the door. The ordinarily unflappable Jeeves was clearly flapped as he exited the limo like a shot.

I laid on the floor trying to catch my breath.

Holy smokes.

I think I get that whole *Twilight* thing now.

NINE

"Fortuna!" Aunt Addie called out before my sneakered foot hit the fancy welcome mat. The older woman dried her hands on a flowered apron. "You've finally come to help us!" Her eyes were shining with all the pent-up hopes she had that I would free her sister's ghost. "Can I get you anything? Herbs, incense? Do you need a wand? Do you *use* a wand?"

"Ms. Otto—"

"Call me Aunt Addie, dear, please, I *insist*," the round woman ushered me further into the house. Martin's aunt, the sister of his deceased mother, looked excited to see me. Until she glanced behind me, a confused expression on her face. "You're not with Martin?"

"No, ma'am," I told her. "Jeeves is actually helping me out with something. We just stopped by the house so he could...um, eat." I glanced toward the kitchen. Jeeves stood near the fridge, gulping down something straight from a large glass milk bottle.

The something in the bottle was dark red.

I shuddered.

Her shoulders slumped, and her excited smile faded. "You're *not* here about the witch bottles, then?" she asked, looking crestfallen before I even answered.

"No, ma'am. I'm still working through what I plan to do about that."

Aunt Addie bit her lip, her eyes filling with tears. She nodded. "I...understand," she replied haltingly, her shaking hands nervously smoothing the already smooth apron again.

But she didn't.

And she didn't believe me.

Which wasn't fair, frankly.

I *had* done some research, but...

There was no documentation of the supposed Mystic's End curse or the witch bottles. Oh, there were *coincidences*, sure—a lot of women seemed to die under mysterious circumstances in this town. Then there were the women at the Holy Grove Church (run by Rev. Dexter Kane), convinced there were magic and devils here. And sure, Spike (who was never around anymore now that he and Liz could chat through a ghost app) couldn't seem to leave the town's limits.

And the stupid magic book I dug up—well, okay, not *dug* up, more like it was flung at me by the earth—had been little help with any of this (seeing as how it was mostly blank).

Except when it criticized me.

Anyway, sure, yeah, there were things afoot here.

So much was afoot that I wasn't about to unleash yet *another* thing so it could stomp around and make matters even worse.

"Miss Addie—"

"Aunt Addie, dear," the woman corrected.

"Right." I nodded. "Look, I'm not saying I'm not going to help you find your sister, and I'm not saying that I won't try and break the bottles. Right now, I'm having a *tough* time trusting people, if you want to know the truth. Jeeves maneuvered me around with that fake urn theft," I waved toward the vampire, now on his second chilled bottle. "Martin didn't tell me why he was sidling up to me, *and* he made me think he was interested in me—"

"Oh my goodness, dear, do you think Martin *pretended* to care about you just to get you to help?" Aunt Addie asked me, shocked.

"How would *I* know?" I held out my arms. "Your family's witch brigade have him trussed up in magical shields like an armored tank going to war. I can't sense much of *anything* from him and let's face it, Aunt Addie—your nephew isn't *exactly* an open book to begin with," I told her. "How can I trust someone that's deliberately hiding things from me?"

Aunt Addie stepped back and eyed me critically. "Well, Miss Fortuna, it seems you've hopped on that entitled train faster than the ocean foam hits the beach, haven't you?"

I blinked. "I'm sorry?"

"Martin told me all about your refusal to use your powers, you know." Aunt Addie crossed her arms. "You don't use your powers most of the time *anyway*. Or so I hear. Why would Martin being protected from psychic probing have *anything* to do with whether or not you trust him? You wouldn't have probed him *anyway*. So why should that matter?"

"That's not the point—"

"Oh, I think it *is*, young lady." Aunt Addie built up a head of steam. "On the one hand, you're a psychic witch, and you could confirm the truth or the lie in any situation you face. On the *other* hand, you won't use any of your powers to do so. Not most of the time. And on the *other* hand—"

"That's *three* hands," I pointed out.

"—you use your own *supposed* ethics as your *reason* not to trust or help people," Aunt Addie finished. "Martin's the son of a mobster and his mother's dead. Just considering those two reasons alone, Fortuna, do you think it was easy for him to open up to you at all? To *anyone*?"

I blinked again. "But he didn't—"

"But he *did*," she declared in a tone that invited no argument.

Jeeves hurried over to us and placed a hand on the unhappy woman's pudgy arm. "Aunt Addie—"

"Don't you *dare*, vampire!" Aunt Addie pushed Jeeves's hand away. "I've been patient long enough. This is my *sister* we're talking about, not just Martin's mother. This affects me, too, and I'm going to have my say. She's *my* kind, and I *have* that right! Don't you dare try and interfere. I've had about enough of that, young man."

"Ma'am," Jeeves answered quietly and then stepped back.

She uncrossed her arms as she faced me, and then crossed them again as if trying to keep them occupied so she wouldn't zap me. "Now, you listen to me, Fortuna Delphi. I don't care if you fall in love with my nephew or that detective or whatever other men you're running around with," Aunt Addie told me fiercely. "Your personal life is *none* of my business. But I am *your* kind, and I need *your* help. I've waited patiently for it. Yes, maybe Martin and Jeeves went about things the wrong way. But so have *you*."

For a long time, I said nothing.

Looking into the eyes of the older woman, I saw pain, anger, and desperation, all competing for prominence there. It was more than that, though. I saw fear. She was afraid that I would refuse them, that her sister would never be free.

"I'm sorry," I told her quietly, but my simple apology did nothing to soften her expression. "You're right, I didn't consider how you would feel sharing your story with me only to have me...turn my back on your plea for my help." I took a deep breath. "Please understand I didn't do it because I was selfish. I'm taking my time because...because I don't fully trust myself yet. As a witch. I don't know that I could handle something bad if I wind up calling it up."

"You don't gain confidence as a witch by living life as a human, by denying *who you are*," Aunt Addie told me firmly. "You don't become a better witch by holding on to your human way of life the way moss clings to a damp wall, Fortuna. At some point, you *have* to let go."

* * *

"Did you know she was going to tear into me like that?"

"Did I know she would say something to you?" Jeeves asked as I sat down in the back of the limo. "I suspected that Aunt Addie would say *something* to you, yes. Did I know she was going to tear into you in that manner? No. It wasn't planned on her part, and so I didn't see it coming until it happened."

"So it was a spontaneous tongue-lashing. Great." I glanced at the time on my phone and looked back at Jeeves. "Okay, let's head over to the shop. We'll be a little early, but maybe I can actually sell something in between now and then."

Jeeves told the driver where we were going and closed the partition again. Turning back to face me, he stared as if seeing me for the first time.

I held up my hands. "What?"

"How do you do that?" he asked curiously.

"How do I do what?"

"Shift gears like that. Take something profound that happens and just push it away as if it doesn't affect you at all."

"It wasn't that profound, first of all. Second, I don't let things rattle me." I shrugged. "A skill I would think you could appreciate."

"Don't you even want to think about what Aunt Addie said? Talk about it?"

"Are we *buddies* now, Sparkles?"

"*There* she is," Jeeves smiled.

"There's *who?* What are you talking about?"

"Whenever things get too personal, you push them away and deflect. You and Martin are far more similar than you might think, Fortuna."

"Yeah, well, maybe it's a side effect of our rich kid upbringing or something," I told him, shrugging. "The simple fact is I don't know what there is to talk about. She was right. Aunt Addie didn't do anything to me or betray my trust, and she asked for my help. I ignored that because I was upset with you and Martin. I just swept her in with everyone else."

"And what she said about you not trusting yourself as a witch?"

"She didn't say that, *I* did," I told him defensively.

"My apologies." His alert, richly colored eyes bore into mine. Jeeves looked healthier now, more human. Well, he looked human before, but more *emo club kid* pale human compared to now. His muscles even looked slightly more prominent, and he positively pulsed with life. "I just wondered what you were going to do to resolve the impasse the two of you seemed to agree on."

"Nothing right now. I need to find this dog and solve the problem in front of me."

"Fortuna, one thing I've learned being Martin's

bodyguard? There is *always* a problem in front of you. You can always find enough of them to fill your time if you want to avoid something. At least *I* can." He smiled, and it struck me just how handsome the vampire was.

Why was *everyone* in this town super hot?

Even shaggy biker Ollie was attractive in his own way.

"Oh, yeah? What are you avoiding?" I asked him.

"Right now? Martin," he said frowning.

"Wait, what?" I leaned forward, shocked at his answer.

"Oh, no," Jeeves laughed, the lines around his eyes creasing so his whole face smiled. "You don't get to turn the tables after you avoided talking about your personal business with me. I'll go as far as you're willing to go—but you *will* go first."

"Why, Sparkles, it sounds like you don't trust me." I fluttered my eyelashes.

"I don't," he answered simply.

"Well, at least we're both clear on where we stand with one another."

* * *

"I'm not talking to you," I told Gideon as Jeeves, and I entered the shop. "Not unless you're ready to talk to me and tell me what happened this morning. Well?"

Gideon barked.

And another, fainter bark from upstairs.

I froze.

"Fortuna, the dog—"

"Don't you tell me!" I shouted at Jeeves, cutting him off. Whirling on Gideon, I faced the smug-looking hound. "*You* tell me. Right now. Gideon, why did I hear another dog bark? Spill it."

Gideon barked.

Another echoed bark from upstairs.

"I swear, dog, if Bella is upstairs and you had *anything* to do with this gigantic mess of a day, I will turn you into a frog." I stormed up the stairs shouting as I went. "I will *withhold* bacon for eternity. I'll turn you into a cat. You want to be a cat, Gideon?"

Gideon barked.

Another bark from upstairs.

"Oh, Gideon, *what* did you do?" I whispered. I hurriedly rounded the corner on the top landing and stared at the fawn-colored greyhound lying lazily across my bed.

My jaw dropped.

Sitting next to the missing greyhound on my bed was a ghost.

And it *wasn't* Spike.

TEN

The ghost watched the greyhound with calm affection. Her meticulously fashionable outfit clung to the living memory of her shapely body. This outfit would have been more at home at a Fashion Week party in New York or Milan than the small Arkansas town of Mystic's End.

"Bella?" Jeeves asked.

Both the dog and the ghost lifted their eyes to meet his.

"I am...and he is..." Bella Grayson's eyes were striking in their intensity, but they held a puzzled look. "Where are we? And who are you?" The ghostly apparition flickered like a candle caught in a stiff breeze. As if she wasn't all there. "Why am I here? Do you know why I am here?" Her voice was calm—as if she was unconcerned by the answers to her questions. Looking down at her delicate hands, she stared. "Why do I look like this?"

Gideon barked. Bella the dog followed with one of his own. The ghost continued to look befuddled.

"Go next door to Liz's and get Spike," I told Jeeves. "Tell him we need him here, pronto."

He nodded and headed swiftly down the stairs.

"Do I know you?" Bella asked, a frightened catch in her throat. The sense of confusion in her face as she examined me tugged at my heart. I'd never spoken to a ghost so soon after their death. Well, not one still confused about what had happened to them.

"No, Mrs. Grayson, you don't know me," I told her softly, stepping forward. "Can you tell me the last thing you remember?"

"I'm dead. Aren't I?" Bella inclined her head toward the window. I glanced out, but could see nothing besides blue sky and fluffy clouds. "That's why I feel so strange. I'm no longer here. And yet, I *am* here." The young woman winced. "Is Petey dead, too?"

I raised an eyebrow. "Petey?"

"My dog." Bella pointed and tried to pat the fawn-colored greyhound on his muscled rump, but her hand passed through it. The sense of confusion in her face grew more pronounced. "Oh, dear," she said. A frown creased her forehead. "Is Petey dead, too?" Bella asked again as if she didn't remember asking me the exact same question just a second ago.

"Bella, can you tell me what you remember?" I asked again without answering.

"Darkness." The ghost shuddered. "Darkness, so much darkness. It was like I was covered in a wet blanket. I tried to move, but I couldn't. I tried to speak, but I couldn't say anything. I couldn't breathe. I was underwater. Or was I? It was like I was underwater. It was so cold. And then I was so far underwater that there was...there was nothing there anymore."

"And after that?"

"Sunshine." A smile crinkled her mouth, her eyes still on Petey. Some of the confusion faded from her eyes. "Warm sunshine coming in through the trees. I was warm again. It was so good to be warm again. And then Petey was there." A wider smile. "He was so happy to see me, he jumped in the air like a puppy." Then another frown. "But I couldn't touch him." She looked up at me. "I'm dead, aren't I?"

"Yes," I told her simply.

"But you can see me. Are you dead?"

"No. My name is Fortuna Delphi, and I'm a witch. I can see ghosts sometimes."

Bella tilted her head forward. "Is Petey dead?"

"No, your dog's fine, Bella. Though the whole town is searching for him at the moment," I told her, giving Gideon a sharp glare. "How did you and Petey wind up here?"

"The trees," she answered simply.

"I'm sorry?" I asked, sure I didn't hear her correctly.

"The trees."

"Did you say *the trees*?"

Bella nodded. "The trees shook one after another, like lights along a path. One would start, we would step and that one would stop only to be followed by the tree after it." Her voice and expression were getting brighter, her ghostly image solidifying as she spoke. "Petey jumped and followed where they pointed. Or lead. Or whatever they were doing." Bella shrugged. "The trees led us here."

"How did you get in?"

"I floated through the door."

"And Petey?"

"He wiggled in through—"

Suddenly Petey and Gideon barked frantically to drown out Bella's answer. I glared sternly at my dog, and his barks trailed off until he was sitting silently, staring. Finally, Petey grew quiet, too.

Once they stopped, Bella tried again.

"Through the—"

The cacophony of barks nearly broke my eardrums. Gideon, the little weasel he was, didn't want me to know how he got in and out of the house.

Bella shrugged.

"You are in so much trouble, dog," I told him.

An image slammed into me of a cartoonish Jeeves running away holding an urn. Then a picture of Gideon running away with Petey.

"What does that have to do with anything?" I asked him.

An image of Martin with a *help wanted* sign. That image flickered out and was replaced by a vision of Bella and Petey with a *help wanted* sign.

"So, you saw how upset I was with Jeeves and Martin for manipulating me to help them." I shook a bewildered head. "And based on that, you decided to do the same type of thing to get me to help here? Help with *what*, Gideon? Azalea's been arrested for kidnapping that dog, and if I call the police and say I found it in my shop? *No* one's going to believe me."

"You were trying to find the dog, anyway," Spike said as he floated in, Jeeves directly behind him. "What difference does it make where you found it? The dog's been found. They have to let Azalea off the hook, right?"

"Or they can say she kidnapped it and stashed it here."

"But she didn't."

"I think Fortuna's concern is that without a believable explanation as to where the dog's been," Jeeves said, turning toward Spike, "the police are unlikely to drop the charges against Miss Cotton. Fortuna's goal was not just to *find* the greyhound, but to offer up an explanation that extricates Miss Cotton from her predicament."

"This didn't *help* anything, Gideon," I told the dog as his tail drooped. "In fact, this *may* have made the whole situation worse."

An image of me holding a ratchet and working to fix something flashed in my mind.

I took a deep, steadying breath and tried to remain calm. Whatever Gideon's opinion of my Ms. Fix-it skills, I didn't know how on earth I would resolve this mess. But now, thanks to it landing in my bedroom?

I had to keep trying.

* * *

Spike and Bella remained upstairs. I was grateful that Spike had become far calmer in the months since I found him. He approached Bella with a gentle sympathy I hadn't realized he was capable of after his multi-year isolation. The time he'd spent rebuilding his friendship with Liz had mellowed him. The ghost displayed an incredible empathy toward the confused Bella, and I felt good leaving her in his hands for now.

Before I'd gone downstairs, I instructed Gideon to remain on the third floor with Petey, and the dog *seemed* to understand. Whether he would actually obey was another issue altogether, but I hoped he realized what was at stake here.

It was *imperative* the greyhound not be seen by anyone until I could figure out what to do.

Jeeves stepped in front of me as we glanced out the storefront window. He turned to face me. "So. Now what?"

The vampire had a good question.

I was trying to think of an answer when Gabe, Pepper, and Ollie walked in.

"We have *not* found the dog." Pepper dropped her backpack on a table.

"*We* have," Jeeves told her.

Pepper's head snapped toward him eagerly. "You *found* the dog?"

"We have. In fact, he's upstairs on the third

floor as we speak. The dog's with his owner, Bella Grayson."

"Wait, Bella's *alive*?" Ollie asked, dumbfounded.

"No, she's not," I told him. "Her *ghost* is here. Bella Grayson is definitely still dead."

"Okay, wait a minute. Is the *dog* alive?" Gabe asked.

"The dog is alive. Bella Grayson is dead. They are both here right now, in my bedroom."

Gabe nodded. "Have you called Clutterbuck?"

"No," I explained to the three what had happened since we parted company, the story that Bella Grayson related about her death and how she wound up in my bedroom—which was the new *in* place for ghosts, apparently. At least this time I didn't have to tear out one of my walls to work it out.

"I don't see the issue," Gabe shrugged. "Just turn him in."

"I can't call Clutterbuck and explain that a ghost and some trees led Petey here. I have nothing to tell the police about why the dog's here *at all*. Not that they would believe, anyway." I took a weary breath. "Considering how fast they went after Azalea because of PeeGrrr, just *having* the dog here? I don't think it's enough—and it *might* even be used as further evidence against her."

"Petey?" Gabe asked.

"That's what Bella calls the dog."

Pepper frowned and dug around in her backpack.

"We *have* to call Clutterbuck," Gabe insisted. "There's no *case* here, Fortuna. Nothing to investigate. And you have a stolen animal in your bedroom. The longer you hold on to Petey, the worse it's going to be for Azalea. And *you*, too, by the way—you have stolen property."

The situation was absurd, but Gabe had a point. If no one stole the dog, there was nothing we could uncover to help Azalea. Suddenly, I realized something.

"We don't know for *sure* no one stole the dog," I told him. "Or, more specifically, *tried* to steal the dog."

"Of course we do. You just said that Bella and Petey met each other in the forest—"

"No, hold on. Fortuna's right," Pepper disagreed with Gabe. "Think about it. We know what Bella said when she and Petey found each other in the woods. We don't know what happened *before* that. Maybe Petey escaped from a kidnapper or thief. *Someone* left that gate open on purpose," Pepper said, shrugging. "They would have to, right? You and I *checked* the enclosure. The dogs could *not* have got out of that secondary fence if the gate hadn't been open. The security footage is clear. They walked out through an open fence. So who opened it? The ghost?"

"Bella wasn't all there when *I* met her," I told Pepper. "Confused, not terribly aware of what happened to her. There's no way she could manipulate physical objects. It's unlikely she could even do that now."

"Okay, so let's say I accept your premise." Gabe glanced between the two of us. "Pepper and I looked at the security footage. There's nothing on the tape. Sure, okay, someone opened the gate. The problem is that gate is touched by the hands of dozens of workers every day going in and out of the fence, so we can't pull fingerprints. How do we find out if someone was back there? Are there cameras? Who would know?"

"Gideon would know," Pepper said. "He was there, wasn't he?"

"But he's a *dog*. Even if he does know, how is he going to tell us?"

I blew the hair out of my eyes. "So, the thing is—"

"Fortuna's got Dr. Doolittle powers," Pepper interrupted (to make sure *she* was the one telling Gabe something *he* didn't know). "She can talk to Gideon, and he can talk to her."

"You can have a *conversation* with animals,"

Gabe deadpanned as if, out of all the things he'd been told I could do so far, *this* stretched his acceptance to the limit. "Like, *talk* to them. And they talk back." His words conveyed not so much wonder as incredulity.

"Not *animals*. Gideon. And not talk with words but images. Kind of. Well, *I* use words," I tried to explain. "He uses images, mostly. Or plays back his memories in my mind to try and get his point across."

"Why just Gideon?"

"Have you ever heard of a witch's familiar?" Pepper asked him. She pointed to me before he could respond. "Gideon's her familiar."

Gabe's brow furrowed. "I thought they were cats? Familiars, I mean."

Pepper rolled her eyes. "If you base your knowledge of witches from accounts of the crusades, maybe."

"If he did *that*, he'd think Gideon was a low-ranking demon," Ollie pointed out.

"I'm not so sure he *isn't*," I muttered under my breath.

Ollie smirked. "What was that?"

"Nothing, nothing."

"While this is all fascinating," Jeeves stepped forward, "if the next step is questioning Gideon, perhaps we should do so. I assume you still plan on talking to the Graysons' lawyer, and time has become a factor—considering the stolen dog is right upstairs."

Gabe turned and stared at Jeeves as if he was surprised he was still here. "What's your interest in all this?"

"I need Fortuna's assistance with a separate matter," the vampire responded without elaborating. "The sooner she is done with all this, the sooner I can obtain that assistance."

"Fine," I said, turning and walking toward the back. "But first, the kitchen."

"Why the kitchen?" Ollie asked.

"I'm going to need at least a pound of bacon for this."

* * *

Gideon smelled the bacon before he saw me. He scrambled off the bed and lunged toward me.

"Oh, no!" I told him, holding up the heaping plate of hot bacon. "You and I are going to have a talk first. For each answer you give me, you get a slice. Understand?"

Gideon frantically jumped on me and pawed at the plate.

"Sit!"

The greyhound did *not* sit.

What's more, the *other* greyhound joined him in his attempts to knock the mound of crispy goodness out of my hand.

"That's it, you two," I said sternly, and I pointed toward the plate. With a whisper, the plate hovered ten feet in the air at the center of the room.

Both hounds whined as if someone was trying to carve off their tails with a rusty knife.

"Okay, Gideon, here we go. Try and keep your answers simple, okay?"

Gideon bark-whine-howled as his body trembled with excitement.

"Was the gate already open? Is that how the two of you got out?"

A sign flashed in my mind. YES MEANS YES. It was an image from the television, a report of a protest we had watched a few days before. The Little Rock local news had covered a college protest on consent. I floated a single slice of bacon down to each dog, and they snatched it from the air in front of them.

"Did he answer you?" Gabe asked.

I nodded. "Yes, the gate was open."

The dogs gathered beneath the floating plate and stared upward with excitement.

"Did he see anyone on the other side of the gate?" Pepper asked.

YES MEANS YES

Another slice of bacon floated down.

"*How* is he answering you?" Gabe asked me curiously.

"I think he somehow can access things I've seen in the way that I see them," I explained while the two dogs wolfed down their reward. "So, he finds something I've seen that correlates to his answer. Occasionally, he can imagine something from things I've seen, but I think it's harder for him, so he doesn't do it often. He can also show me things *he's* seen, but that's not super useful."

"Why not?"

"Dogs don't see the world the same way we do,." Bella Grayson looked over at the excited hounds. "Their vision is quite different, the colors they see. And a greyhound's vision is different from other dogs', as well."

"He can't hear you," I told Bella, and then repeated to Gabe what she said.

"Bella Grayson is here now?" he asked, looking around.

I nodded and refocused on Gideon. "Gideon, the person you saw—was he or she waiting for Petey?"

YES MEANS YES

Bacon.

"Did they try to grab Petey, or get him on the lead?"

YES MEANS YES

Bacon.

"Can you show me what they looked like?"

YES MEANS YES

I waited.

Gideon waited.

"Show me what he looked like, Gid."

The dog thrust an image into my mind...of bacon.

I rolled my eyes and gave the two dogs their treat.

Once they finished, a blackish and yellow image of boots stomping in the grass exploded into my mind. The growl of two dogs, and then a yelp, and then the taste of filthy denim. The acrid smell of cigarettes mixed with freshly cut grass. Then the thundering sound of paws racing into the forest, a voice cursing after them.

Dogs hear twice as many frequencies as humans, so I couldn't identify it, much less tell whether it was a man or a woman. The sound he sent barely sounded human in my mind.

I lowered the plate between the two hounds (which they attacked) and frowned. *Something* was going on.

But *what*?

ELEVEN

"So, while you were off finding dogs in your bedroom and *doubling* your haunt capacity, I was digging in." Pepper piled papers on the kitchen table. "Now, there were two paths I went down." Pepper smiled brightly at Ollie. He winked back at her. "One, Bella's murder. Two, the other Bella's kidnapping and the whole PeeGrrr thing."

"Petey," I told her absently.

"Who's Petey?"

"That's what Bella called the greyhound. I guess *Bella* was his racing-name nickname or something? Probably because it was so long. I don't know. But calling the dog Petey and the ghost Bella seems like it'll be less confusing."

"Right." Pepper nodded and scribbled something in her pad. "Okay, so let's start with PeeGrrr. There are about forty members, give or take, here in Mystic's End. At least as far as I can tell from their forums on the internet." Her face creased into a scowl. "Membership rolls are private, so I—we—dug into what we could. Anyway, it's a nationwide organization, and it's not really known for terroristic type activities."

"What is it known for?" Gabe asked her.

"Organizing protests and boycotts. And being *very* effective." The reporter pulled out a stack of papers and pointed. "That's seventeen greyhound tracks PeeGrrr has closed down all over the country, and two *states* where they succeeded in getting greyhound racing completely banned."

"Jeeves, you have to have heard of these folks." I gave a brief look at the all-business vampire.

"I've heard of them, of course, but they're not an organization Martin ever seemed *particularly* concerned about." He picked up the stack of papers Pepper had and flipped through them. "These are smaller tracks that generate revenue almost exclusively from greyhound racing."

"Like the track was? Before you guys built the place up, I mean," Pepper said.

"The Complex has a *much* more diverse income stream," he told us, nodding. "Only thirty percent of the people coming ever bet on a race at all. While it's an important aspect of our income and the racing being made illegal would certainly be a blow, it wouldn't be an *unrecoverable* one. A greater percentage of people play the slot machines at the casino."

"Then why bother at all?" I asked him. He looked at me curiously, eyebrow raised. "There's definitely an argument to be made that the dogs shouldn't be exploited the way they're being exploited, right? I mean, PeeGrrr has a point. If you could survive without it, why not just stop doing it altogether?"

"Thirty-percent is still a fairly large amount of money, Fortuna."

I stared at him, a pained frown on my face. "It always comes down to money."

"It's not my decision," Jeeves responded.

"So, you *are* right about one thing," Pepper said, pulling out another piece of paper. "It does always come down to money. That dog is insured for $75,000. Because Ella had to race to sell the dog, she *only* got $45,000 for him from a buyer in Florida." Pepper added a photocopy of a bill of sale to the stack. "Now, on top of Ella's insurance on the dog? Jeff Abernathy *also* has insurance on the dog for *another* $75,000."

I stared at the paper in confusion. "But both of

those policies can't pay out, can they?"

"They can, and they do," Ollie told me with a sly smile. "But they don't pay out the same people."

"I don't understand."

Gabe leaned down to pick up the papers. "This one pays Ella Grayson," he said as he held up one page. "This one pays Jeff Abernathy."

"And this one," Ollie pulled out a third paper and waved it, "covers the buyer in Florida if anything happens to the dog in transport."

"So, wait a minute," I said, calculating. "You mean to tell me that the sale of the dog was $45,000, and Ella *has* that. And if something happens to the dog—"

"Missing, damaged, or dead," Ollie interjected.

"That $45,000 is *added* to $75,000? And *another* $75,000?"

"So Petey missing, damaged or dead is worth $195,000 doled out to three different people."

"Not entirely." Gabe scanned the papers. "The total is $240,000 if you count the fact that Ella *has* the $45,000 from his sale already. This policy covers the reimbursement of that so she won't have to." Gabe frowned as he scanned the paperwork. He looked up at Pepper. "Where did you get these?"

"Oh, Gabe, Gabe, Gabe," she crooned with a sly smile. "You *know* I'll never tell you that. Just accept that I'm better at your job then you are, and we can all move on."

"My job requires me to follow the law."

"Does it, though?" She fixed him with a judgmental stare. "Does it *really*?"

The front door bells jingled from below.

"Give me a minute," I told the group as I moved toward the stairs, thinking about the policies that Pepper uncovered. Maybe it was normal to have so many policies on a racing greyhound, I thought to myself. Perhaps I was placing too much emphasis on the fact that the dog seemed to be worth far more maimed or dead than alive. But that couldn't be true, could it? He was a champion racer.

Still, it seemed...wrong. Calculated.

But maybe it was just a coincidence.

I frowned.

Or maybe the two situations in front of me—the dog disappearing and Bella's death—weren't so separate after all.

* * *

Jeff Abernathy stood downstairs, holding the unfinished portrait of *Bella Bailout X Three Peat Ingathered*, also known as Petey.

Also known as the missing dog sitting in my bedroom with his ghost owner.

"Here." He scowled and shoved the portrait over the counter at me. I noticed the wet paint had been smeared. Dirt caked along the bottom. I sighed as I took it from him. "You left this."

"Well, it's *ruined* now." I cast an irritated glower in his direction. "You could have just tossed it out once the dirt got all over it. No need to come all the way back into town to return it."

Why *was* he here? The man had made it clear he didn't want to hire me. He said he didn't care about the painting for any other reason than he was under contractual obligation to provide it. I didn't finish the art, so he didn't owe me any money for it.

"I ain't *paying* for that thing," Mr. Abernathy told me with gruff defiance. "I wanted to make that clear. Face to face."

"Our contract said payment would be made when the portrait was delivered *finished*, Mr. Abernathy. Obviously, I wouldn't have charged you for a half-finished painting."

He stared at me, his face pinched and angry. "You know, you got a mouth on you, Delphi."

"Everyone has a mouth on them, Abernathy," I responded indifferently, surprised my answer provoked such animosity in him. "I didn't mean anything by what I said, though. I'm sorry if you took offense."

So.

I *wasn't* really sorry that he took offense.

There was nothing for him to take offense over —well, okay, *until* I dropped the honorific. I admit *that* was a little snotty. But *he* did it first. Anyway, truth be told—I didn't care if this guy took a long walk off a short pier as long as he didn't have a greyhound on a lead when he did it.

The guy was rich, entitled scum.

"I don't get the sense you're sorry about much, Delphi." Jeff Abernathy leaned forward on the counter. Scrutinizing me, he continued. "I don't understand why so many of the top men in the town are so fascinated with ya—"

The top men? Was there a *Most Eligible Bachelors of Mystic's End* list I missed?

"—Martin Salvi, Dexter Kane—"

"*Dexter Kane?*" I asked, creeped out at the thought.

Ollie's father, the local preacher, seemed *anything* but fascinated by me. Okay, sure, he leered at me once when he came to get a portrait for Hugh Maddox, but I didn't get the sense that the leer was about *me* so much as the standard way he treated all women.

"He talks about you, you know," Jeff said, his grizzled, unshaven face bouncing in a nod.

"No, I did not know." And I did not care to know, but too late now.

"I don't follow all that religious mumbo jumbo claptrap he goes on and on about. I sit in the pew on Sunday because he's a good friend to have in this town, you know?" Mr. Abernathy eyed me suspiciously. "But he seems to think you showing up here was some kinda sign. Goes on and on about it like you're the second coming or somethin'."

I didn't know what to say. It was the first I'd heard about it.

"First time in the town," I lied. "I'm not the second coming of anything, Mr. Abernathy."

"As for Martin? Well, we *all* know what you're givin' Martin to make *him* sniff after you," the man winked knowingly.

I blushed hotly even though what the man implied wasn't truthful in the slightest. "Mr. Abernathy, *why* are you still here?"

Abernathy leaned forward and exhaled, his foul breath washing over me. "Young lady, I go where *I* want in this town. I was here *long* before you, and I'll be here long after you. But since you asked," he leaned even closer, and I tensed as his invasion of my space went from rude to threatening. "You *didn't* see anything this morning that you didn't tell the police, did you? Something you maybe *forgot* to mention?"

I blinked. "Like what?"

"Well, now, how would *I* know what you

might've seen?" His eyes narrowed as he searched my face for some indication of whatever he expected to find there.

And then I felt it.

A flash of fear.

"Mr. Abernathy, have you contacted the insurance company yet?" I asked slowly. "You spoke about a policy this morning. How much does that pay out *if* they can't find the greyhound?"

He pulled his head back abruptly.

"Is there a reason," I continued casually, "that you're *here* returning a painting to save a few hundred dollars instead of, oh, I don't know—out in the forest scouring for Petey?"

At the mention of the dog's informal pet name, Jeff Abernathy went pale.

"I have Hoyt and the other hands looking for that dog," he answered quickly. Too quickly. "Are you implying I'm not trying to look for the dog, Miss Delphi? That *I* know what happened to it? Huh?"

I raised an eyebrow. "I didn't say anything of the sort, Mr. Abernathy. I *do* wonder why *you* did, though. Is there any reason I should think you know what happened to Petey, Mr. Abernathy?" I leaned forward. "Tell me something. How well *do* you know Ella Grayson, anyway?"

Jeff Abernathy turned on his heel and stormed

out of my shop so quickly that he almost ran over Chief Clutterbuck.

The Chief reached out and steadied the angry man, Jeff Abernathy—who was waving in my direction. The two men exchanged a few words, and then the elder Abernathy turned again and walked swiftly to the right. Clutterbuck turned toward me, glared through the window, and then walked casually toward the left.

I walked to the front of my shop and locked the door, flipping around the closed sign.

As usual.

* * *

"That was *fascinating*," Pepper said when I returned to the second floor. She was shoving a massive black thing back in her bag. It had wires trailing all the way to the floor.

"Are you all right?" Gabe asked, his eyes dark with concern.

"How do you all know what went on downstairs?" I asked them, confused. The stairs to the second floor were in the back room of the building, two rooms away from the storefront.

"I didn't *think* she knew about the bug," Ollie admonished Pepper with a frown. "Not cool, Pep."

I didn't even have to ask. I knew it instantly.

"You *bugged* my shop?" I gaped at her. My friend refused to meet my eyes. "Pepper Stanford, did you *bug* my shop?" When she didn't answer, I walked around the table and yanked the bag out of her hand. Opening it, I stared at a black box marked SPY MASTER 30000. "You have *got* to be kidding me."

"Look, it came in handy, didn't it?"

"You will take *every last bug* out of my shop."

"Okay, okay, fine," Pepper grumbled, rolling her eyes.

"I meant *now*, Pepper. You will take every last bug out of my shop *right now*."

She stared at me, her face belligerently defensive. With a calculating pause, Pepper waited. I pointed and was treated to yet another roll of her eyes. "Fine. But don't you dare talk about anything without me!" As she stomped down the stairs, Gabe turned to me.

"Did he look as suspicious as he sounded from up here?"

"More," I told him. "Something happened this morning that he *thinks* I could have seen, and he was seriously afraid of it. That I saw it, I mean. I think the whole visit was just to intimidate me."

"From what I heard, *that* backfired on him," Ollie joked.

"He turned *completely* pale when I mentioned

Petey's pet name, too. Like, snow-white blood-draining-to-his-toes kind of pale."

"He didn't expect you to know that," Gabe said.

"You're talking without me!" Pepper hollered, racing back up the stairs.

"You deserve it," Ollie told her caddishly. "You bugged your best friend."

"Okay, *hacker*," Pepper retorted, referencing Ollie's hobby of breaking into computer systems for fun and curiosity. "What *do* we think about the conversation?"

"We think we want to know what Jeff thinks she saw," Gabe said.

"That's easy. Fortuna, do your fidget-finger thing with the painting." My friend pulled me toward the stairs. "Make the things you saw go in the painting, and we can all take a look. See if we see anything suspicious."

"That's not a bad idea," I admitted, moving to follow her. A light hand on my arm stopped me, and I turned to find Jeeves looking at me intently. "What?"

"I know that time is of the essence, but I did want to bring up the fact that your home may still be bugged. Since the idea seems to bother you a great deal, I thought I would—"

"Hey! Back off, Sparkles," Pepper snapped at him angrily. "I took every bug out of her shop!"

"Yes, no doubt you took every listening device out of her *shop*," Jeeves agreed coolly. "Fortuna asked you to take every listening device out of her *shop*, and I have no *doubt* that you complied with her request *exactly*." Jeeves looked down at me. "You did, however, *only* ask her to remove the devices from your *shop*. You did not inquire as to whether she bugged the second or third floors."

"She knew what I meant," I told the vampire. I turned and looked at Pepper. "Right?"

Pepper's eyes wandered everywhere but toward me.

"Pepper?"

"Sorry, what?" She stared at me with a practiced innocence. Then a friendly smile.

"Do you have more bugs in my building?" I stared.

"Ew, Fortuna, how would *I* know if you have bugs in your building?" she responded, shuddering. "There's a *great* exterminator just down the—"

"Pepper!"

"Oh, fine!" Pepper shouted with exasperation. She stomped toward the table and ran her hand underneath. "And *you*, vampire? I don't like *you* anymore."

"Your affection was never required, so that's perfectly fine," Jeeves answered.

Pepper rolled her eyes so much lately I was seriously surprised they didn't fall out of her head.

TWELVE

I was so annoyed at Pepper that Gabe and I headed over to the lawyer's office before I *fidget-fingered* my art all over her face. Well, that and discovering what the legal situation was *might* help me figure out what to focus on when I did recreate what I'd seen.

The attorney's building was not far from my own, located just off the town square on a road that could have been mistaken for an alley. A small wooden sign flapped over a door that could have been confused with the back entrance to one of the larger storefronts facing the center of town. BARBARA TOWNSEND, ATTORNEY AT LAW

I pushed open the door and peeked into the one-room office.

Considering the purported wealth of the Graysons, Barbara Townsend's office was *not* what I expected.

Calculators, pens, paper pads were strewn about haphazardly. Most pens bore teeth marks as if the owner had anxiously chewed her way through every case. The smell of stale coffee hung in the air, and half-drunk mugs were strewn about. The scent of coffee was *almost* strong enough to overpower the odor of the musty carpet...but not quite. Three cats splayed lazily in small shafts of sunlight that peeked through the dirty windows.

A tiny woman sat dwarfed behind a large wooden desk, her curly hair frizzed as if she had just washed it but forgot to choose a style for the day. A sprinkling of freckles covered her cheeks and nose, making her seem too young to be a practicing lawyer. Thick glasses dominated her face in a frame that wouldn't have been out of place in the nineteen-fifties.

"Ms. Townsend?" I asked, causing her to jump.

"Oh! Oh, sorry. Sorry, didn't hear you," the woman responded. She spoke rapidly, almost frantically, pushing the frizzy mop of hair back from her face. "No one really comes here anymore. Not since my Dad died a couple of years ago." The young woman gestured toward a prominent portrait on the wall. "I'm lucky to have any clients at all if you want to know the truth. Which you don't, do you? I mean, you *do*. Just not about this. You're not lost, right? The Graysons sent you? Or you're lost. Are you lost?"

I moved into the small room so Gabe could enter in after me. Barbara Townsend's eyes widened.

"Gabe!" the small woman blushed hotly and jerked her head to pull her hair back into her face. "They didn't tell me *you* would be coming." Barbara hopped up from her chair and swept piles of papers and files off the single chair sitting in front of her desk. They cascaded haphazardly onto the floor.

"I'm sorry, do we know each other?" Gabe asked politely as he pulled a chair from a beat-up conference table next to the one the lawyer had prepared for him. He gestured for me to sit down.

The lawyer fixed Gabe with an anguished look. "You don't remember me?" Barbara's voice had a grating, nasal twang, and I found it hard to believe *anyone* could forget her. "We were in fifth-grade band together! You sat in front of me."

"Um, of *course*, of course," Gabe lied smoothly and smiled at the tiny, awkward woman. "How could I forget? I haven't seen you in ages, Barbara? How have you been?"

"My father died," she repeated and pointed again at the portrait that stared over the room judgmentally. "I never wanted to be a lawyer, but I guess it was a good thing I did since he, you know, died." Barbara seemed more resentful than mournful discussing her deceased father. "My mom needs the money from the firm. I do okay." Barbara shrugged and sat down behind the gigantic desk again.

"Well, your legal acumen is why we're here," I broke in.

"My what? Did you call me inhuman?" Barbara looked at me, confused. "And who are *you*?"

"Barbara, I assume the Graysons told you about the fact that Bella's dog is missing," Gabe said, his crystal-blue eyes fixed on the attorney. Gabriel Wilcox turned his southern charm up by a factor of at *least* ten. At least. "They implied that you might have access to information that could help us."

"I have so much information, it'd make your head explode into tiny little pieces of multi-colored confetti, babe—um, Gabe," Barbara told us with a bitter grimace. She got up and slid open a file cabinet door, grabbed a handful of folders, and returned to the desk, leaving the drawer hanging open. "I don't know what happened with poor

Bella Grayson, but I can tell you that girlfriend of hers—"

"Excuse me, did you say girlfriend?" I interrupted.

"I did," Barbara nodded.

"I thought Ella Grayson was Bella's wife?"

"So did she, apparently," the attorney snorted. "Rude awakening when she found out she was wrong."

"I don't understand," Gabe said.

"Gay marriage was legal in New York, right?" Barbara said. "But Ella and Bella didn't get married in New York. They got a *domestic partnership*. That's *only* valid in New York, so when they moved here? It didn't mean anything."

"But they called each other wife, didn't they?" I asked.

Barbara nodded. "Sure did. And Ella Grayson stormed in here before poor Bella was even transferred to the crematory *demanding* that I help her get everything in her name alone." She flipped through the files and pulled out a sheet of handwritten notes. "Ella claimed her New York lawyer told her that when she moved, all the two of them had to do was represent themselves as wives. *Then* live together. Then say they're married to everyone else. And they would be common-law married."

"Well, they *did* that, didn't they?"

"They *did*, they sure did," Barbara agreed and nodded. "But not in *Texas*. The two of them had *originally* planned to move to Austin, and everything that fancy New York lawyer told Bella? That would have been true in the state of *Texas*. The state of *Arkansas*? We don't have common-law marriage. At all. Apparently," the woman snorted, "I was the first person to tell Ella stick-up-her-butt *that*."

"How'd she take the news?" Gabe asked.

"Well, Detective, to say she melted down right here in my office? That'd be an understatement." Barbara Townsend pointed to the corner where gray dust and broken pottery lay. "She threw Daddy at me. Luckily, I'm pretty quick, and I jumped out of the way. Can't say Daddy was as lucky."

Gabe glanced at the shattered urn and shuddered. "So, what happens now?"

"Now, Detective, I finish writing this up"—she pointed to her old computer—"to get Ella's claws out of the Grayson family's inheritance."

"I thought Bella had a will leaving her everything?" I asked.

"She did. And three weeks ago?" More shuffling of papers. Finally, Barbara Townsend held up a single page and waved it at us. "She *changed* it."

* * *

"Your friend Claire was left Petey," Gabe said, walking and scanning the will while I guided him back toward the shop. "Ella was left absolutely *nothing*. The house, art, money in the bank accounts that Ella wasn't on, it all went to Claire. All of it. I wonder what happened three weeks ago that caused Bella to do all this?"

"I can ask her when we get back," I murmured. Suddenly, a leather-clad man leaving the center courthouse building caught my attention. His hair was black-blue, and I could swear I could see guyliner on his eyes, even from this distance. He glanced around as if concerned about who was watching. "Hey, who's that?" I pointed.

Gabe squinted. "I don't know, actually. He looks *vaguely* familiar, but I can't quite place him."

His lumbered walk was swift and deliberate moving through the crisscrossing sidewalks. His black leather pants, jacket, and motorcycle boots looked out of place in the country square. Two women sitting on benches grabbed the hands of their children and pulled them tight as he came closer. With a swift motion, he opened the back of a waiting limousine himself and hopped in.

"Is that a casino limo?" I asked Gabe.

"I think so."

"What would a *tourist* be doing at the town courthouse?"

"That's the *old* courthouse," Gabe reminded me. "Nothing there but obsolete archives. And that guy doesn't look like a historian."

"How obsolete?" I asked him.

"Well, most records are in the big county building," Gabe said. "That's city stuff like City Council transcripts, city bills, that kind of stuff. There's also a floor that has really old historical archives from hundreds of years ago. The state handles most public records, so there's just not a huge amount of stuff kept in there anymore. Heck, the police department keeps the city police archives in that cage at the library. Other than the old jail in the basement? There just isn't much there unless you're a historian."

"I didn't even know the place was open," I said as we walked by. "I never see anyone go in."

"No one really does," Gabe shrugged. "But it's the center of town and a historic building. We should use it for something, but we really don't."

I glanced at the building once more before we went into my shop.

* * *

"They *weren't* married?" Pepper was aghast. "How did *you* find that out before *me*?"

We stood in the art studio as Gabe related what we learned.

"You're slipping?" Gabe shrugged nonchalantly. "You and Ollie dating has taken the edge off? You need to be frustrated and unhappy to do really great work? I don't know. Could be any number of things."

Pepper stared at him, goggle-eyed.

"Hey, dude, chill," Ollie told Gabe with a bemused look. "I know you two have your history and all, but she's *kinda* my girlfriend now, and I don't want to have to fight you or challenge you to a duel or something to defend her honor. That'd be a real downer."

"I'm *kind of* your girlfriend?" Pepper gave Ollie a menacing look.

"Babe, you know I don't like absolutes." He stared back with an ain't-I-irresistible smile. "We haven't talked about it, but you know how I feel and all. I didn't wanna speak for you."

Jeeves stared silently at the group, looking like he wanted to be *anywhere* but here.

"I absolutely think we're getting closer." Pepper ignored Ollie's charming grin, and snatched the will out of Gabe's hands. Scanning, she frowned. "Ella got absolutely nothing. If *this* is the will, how is she running around selling off all of Bella's stuff?"

"Barbara told us that Bella asked her to hold off on filing it until she could talk to Ella," I said.

"And that was *when?*"

"Within days of her death," Gabe said. "She died two weeks ago, she asked this be changed three weeks ago. But she never followed up with Barbara to officially file it."

"And you *seriously* wonder why I think that your department is completely corrupt?" Pepper asked him. "*How* did they miss this? Or did they just ignore it?"

"Are you saying this was covered up on purpose?"

"Well, was it?"

"Ask *your* maybe-boyfriend," Gabe pointed at Ollie. "It was *his* boss that classified her death as totally natural. If the coroner says a death was natural, as far as we're concerned, the death is natural. No one contacted us to say otherwise."

"Right, but no one contacted you to say otherwise because Bella's entire family was conveniently halfway across the world at the time of her death," I pointed out.

"We're just going over the same points we already know." Gabe rubbed his forehead. "This is all suspicious, but none of it is proof of anything. It's all circumstantial."

Pepper rolled her eyes.

"A drug overdose isn't circumstantial," Ollie disagreed.

Pepper added, "Oh, come on, Gabe. It's *obvious* Ella killed Bella!"

"Obvious isn't *proof*, Pepper. *How* many times do I have to tell you that?"

"And how many times do I have to tell you to *respect the chain* of command, *Detective?*"

We froze as soon as the unexpected voice boomed from the front of the shop.

"Chief Clutterbuck," I said cheerily, meeting him in the doorway. "Is there something I can help you with?"

How the heck had he got in with none of us hearing the bells?

"Yes, Miss Delphi, you can stop roping my detective into your shenanigans." His voice was low and accusatory as he stared at me with contemptuous resentment.

Suddenly, a dog barked from upstairs.

And then another, distinctly different dog barked.

Crap.

"Ms. Delphi, do you have—"

"Chief Clutterbuck, I'm not open," I said,

cutting him off and pointing toward the closed sign in my front window. The suspicious, angry chief didn't turn to check. "Unless you have a warrant? You're not welcome here. Now, please leave."

Clutterbuck's eyes narrowed dangerously as his gaze traveled from face to face to face. Everyone in the room stared back at him, their blank faces revealing nothing. Finally, he settled back on me with a cold-eyed stare. "Are you sure that's how you want to play this, Miss Delphi?"

"I don't know what you mean, sir." I stared back.

"Gabriel Wilcox?" he asked, his eyes boring into mine.

"Sir?"

"You're fired, son. Turn in your gun and badge by the end of business." Clutterbuck paused for a reaction, but we all remained silent. After a few moments, he smiled coldly. "Y'all have a nice day now."

With a tip of his hat and a cocky wink, the chief of the Mystic's End Police Department turned and left.

THIRTEEN

"Gabe, I'm *so* sorry." Pepper reached out for Gabe, but he pulled away from her. I didn't blame him, to be honest. Her tone *didn't* sound apologetic in the slightest. In fact, she was having trouble covering her smile. "What are you going to do now?"

"Turn in my gun and badge. If the chief meant it, anyway." Gabe's eyes sought mine. "*Did* he?"

"I wasn't trying to read him, but it felt like he meant it. At least from what I could tell."

"Maybe it's time," Gabe sighed. He sat down on the chair with a thump. The detective—er, former detective—looked resigned to what had just occurred, as if this moment had been expected all along. "It's been getting harder to deal with what goes on at the department. I felt this coming, you know."

"Did you?" Jeeves asked.

Gabe nodded and looked across the table at Ollie. "Ollie knows."

"Used to be different. All the mess ups and weird decisions were explained, you know?" Ollie told Jeeves as he shifted forward. "Might have been a lie, but they still tried to pretend things were justified. Now, it's like they're saying the quiet parts out loud."

"You should become a private investigator!" Pepper burst out.

"A private eye?" Gabe looked at me as if waiting for me to say something. I shrugged. "It's not that easy to become a private eye in Arkansas, Pepper. Before you even apply, you have to work for *two years* alongside a licensed private investigator. There *aren't* any in Mystic's End, and I'm not moving away from my grandmother at this point in her life. I'd also really prefer not to commute to Little Rock."

"There sure *are* private dicks in Mystic's End!" Pepper said brightly, and she smiled at Jeeves.

Jeeves stared back at Pepper like a deer caught in the headlights. Well, more like a resentful stag caught in headlights—who was trying to decide whether to ram the car with his immense antlers.

"You're a licensed private investigator?" Gabe asked, surprised.

"I am," Jeeves said, turning.

"But you're a *vampire*."

"They didn't ask whether I was human on the application," Jeeves responded. "I presume that wasn't considered an important qualifier in the licensing process."

"You worked for another private eye for two years?" I asked, curious.

"Private security, private investigation," Jeeves shrugged. "It's all related in most states. Martin's family has several licensed investigators on the payroll, so it wasn't hard to get the experience on paper."

"As much as I *appreciate* everyone's concern about my future, if you all think Clutterbuck left for good, you'd be wrong." Gabe rubbed the back of his neck. "He heard Petey bark upstairs. I'd guess he went straight from here to a judge to get a warrant. We're still in the middle of this case, and that dog is *still* missing and presumed stolen."

"He saw everyone here." My brow wrinkled. "No one in this room can hide the dog. Well, not for long, anyway."

"What about Liz?" Pepper asked, referencing our friend next door.

"She's open, has clients, *and* employees," Gabe

said, shaking his head. "We'd never hide him. Someone would see. Besides, I think we should get him a bit further away from here than next door. Just to be safe."

"How many people actually *know* a greyhound is missing, though?" I asked. Gabe, Pepper, and Ollie looked at me with mildly amused expressions —as if my naïveté regarding gossip in this town was *adorable*. I glanced back at the front door with worry and then turned back. "Okay, then what about Claire? That's who Bella wanted the dog to go to, anyway."

"How do we explain giving the dog to her?" Ollie asked.

"We'll just tell her what happened," I shrugged.

"Can we tell her *all* of what happened?" Ollie glanced meaningfully at Gabe. Pepper reached out and jabbed him. For a moment, I was confused, and then I remembered—*everyone* in this room knew about Miss Bessie being a witch. But Miss Bessie never told Gabe *or* Claire, and so *we* never told Gabe or Claire. That meant Gabe and Claire, at times, had no idea a paranormal drama swirled around them.

"What was that look?" Gabe asked Ollie suspiciously.

"We'll tell her what we can," I shrugged. "Let's leave out the part about Bella floating around next to the dog. It's one thing to know about ghosts. It's another thing entirely to know that a loved one is floating next to you, and you can't see them or talk to them."

* * *

"I don't understand." Claire scratched her cheek and stared at the dog.

Claire's apartment was small. The ceilings were low, and the windows were grimy on the outside, as if diesel trucks continuously spewing black smoke parked just beneath the second floor walk-up. A small window air conditioning unit sputtered as it tried to cool the room—and failed.

Everything about the place was dark despite Claire's apparent attempt to brighten it up with pastel paintings and white accents everywhere. The curtains, though threadbare, were clean and ironed.

As Pepper attempted to explain again, I noticed Gabe looked uncomfortable. He glanced around the studio as if just realizing how little the salary he paid Claire could buy. We had all gone, and we were all packed in like sardines—it only highlighted *how* tiny the place was.

Thank goodness Spike and Bella stayed back at my place to see what the cops did if they actually did show up. The ghosts would have had to share space with people, and that would have just looked weird.

"Fortuna." Jeeves touched my elbow. I stepped away from the group as much as I could, though distance was hard to get in an apartment this tiny. "I just received a text from Martin. He's asked that we —you and I—return to the greyhound track. He found something."

"What?"

"He didn't say."

"About what?"

"He didn't say."

I stared at him. "Did you *ask* him?"

Jeeves bristled at my question. "As I said, I've been asked to return to the track with you," he said tightly.

"Right, I forgot about your *indebted servitude* thing." The struggling air conditioner, shut windows, and the number of people shoved in such a tiny space made me feel claustrophobic. No wonder Claire worked so much at the old folks' home. It was a much more lively place than this. "We'll go in a minute."

"You're going?" Gabe asked, overhearing.

"Martin found something."

"I thought you were going to do your fidget-finger thing with the paint?" he frowned.

"That was before you got fired, and before

Clutterbuck threatened to get a warrant for my place," I pointed out. "Maybe it's not a dog, but if they find paintings of the scene this morning? It might look suspicious. Besides, I know they're all rallying around the supposed missing dog, but I think the dog just tipped us off to a much bigger conspiracy going on. And if there *is* a conspiracy, evidence of that might be at the track."

"I'll come with you, then." Gabe stepped forward.

"Martin was quite specific that he *only* wanted to see Fortuna and me," Jeeves told him. He stepped forward tentatively and wound up smashed between Gabe and me. There didn't seem enough room for the step-up impact statement the vampire was silently *trying* to make, so he just looked the ex-cop directly in the eye. Gabe's jaw flexed as he stared back, his posture stiff.

"Yeah, I *bet* he was," Gabe mocked the vampire.

My chest tightened as the two ratcheted up their cold-war tension. I could feel fury and resentment churning in Gabe—though, to be fair, Gabe had a hard day, and Jeeves's monumental ego seemed to annoy him on a regular day. The vampire was a convenient repository for the anger the terminated cop was trying to stuff down.

I cleared my throat. "Look, Martin will talk more freely if it's just us, anyway. You need to run by the station and turn in your badge and gun before Clutterbuck makes up *impersonating a police officer* charges against you."

Gabe tore his eyes from Jeeves and stared at me, surprised. His spine was as straight as a pencil, and his determined face tensed with anger. I could *feel* the frustration within him like a building storm. It was fed by the desire to argue with me that the department he had given so much to would *never* do something like that to him—but he couldn't.

That he couldn't broke his heart. Just a little.

"Fine," he nodded once.

"But what about the wake this afternoon?" Claire asked. "I can't leave the poor dog in here all alone."

"Wait a second," I said to Jeeves and Gabe. "Claire, *what* wake?"

"The Graysons are having a wake for Bella this afternoon and evening," she said, stretching to the right so she could look at me over Pepper's shoulder. "Since Ella didn't have one, they wanted to make sure her friends and family would be able to mourn together."

"Is it at Holy Grove Church?"

"Oh, goodness, no." Claire shook her head, frowning. "That's *not* their church. It'll be at their house."

"I feel like this day has already been *three* days long," I mumbled.

"It's only four-thirty," Gabe told me.

"In the morning?" I asked sarcastically.

"*I* will go to the wake with Claire," Pepper announced. "Ollie can stay here with Petey in case he needs food or water or a walk. Gabe, *you* go close out your career at the police department. Jeeves and Fortuna can find out what Martin wants. That works for everyone?" Everyone in the group nodded, though Gabe did so reluctantly. "Later tonight, let's meet back at Fortuna's. Say ten or so? We can all compare notes."

"We'll try to make it to the wake if we can," Jeeves told her.

"Me, too? At Fortuna's, I mean?" Claire asked. She reached out and hugged the dog, tears escaping from her eyes as if she didn't even know they were falling.

"You mourn, hon," I said quietly. "We'll find out what happened to your friend."

Claire nodded, and Petey licked the tears from her face with a loud slurp.

* * *

"So, why are you angry at Martin?" I asked Jeeves as we sat in the back of yet another limousine.

"Who said I was angry at Martin?" His expression was stony and guarded

I hated the habit he had of answering a question with another question—or just refusing to answer at all.

"You did. Well, not outright. But that's what it *sounded* like before when we were talking."

Distant thunder rumbled, and I gazed out the window quickly. Storm clouds gathered over the peaks of the Ouachitas—a usual thing for this time of year. The mountains actually affect the climate of Arkansas, though lots of folks didn't know that. Humid winds from the Gulf of Mexico rise as they cross the ridges, and as the winds cool, the air condensed into clouds, fog, or rain.

The forests and mountains of Arkansas could be strange.

Mystic's End fit right in, I guess.

"I disagreed with his decision to call the police on Azalea when she returned," Jeeves responded.

Well, that wasn't the answer I was expecting. "Why?"

"I believed she was innocent."

"Hold the phone there, Sparkles," I turned away from the window and stared at the vampire. I could feel my face flush red with anger. "You've known all day that she was innocent? And this is the *first* you've said anything to me?"

"I didn't say I *knew* she was innocent," Jeeves corrected, looking me up and down. There was no defensiveness in his response or so much as a twitch of a reaction to my anger. "I said I *believed* that the girl was innocent. Due to that, I felt calling the police to take her into custody was premature."

"So why did Martin turn her in?"

Jeeves looked away.

"Sparkles, you *started* down the path. You may as well keep walking."

"I told you once. I'm not going to betray Martin. Not for you, not for anyone."

My eyes narrowed. "What do you mean 'betray' him?" I could hear myself getting accusatory, and I tried to tell myself to cool it. Jeeves and Martin had a strange relationship, and I could understand Martin's machinations better by keeping Jeeves at least somewhat loyal to me.

If I jumped on him every time he said something I didn't like about Martin? I would lose whatever benefit I was getting from making him an ally.

Okay, ally-*ish*.

"Explaining to you why he did what he did would mean I'd have to divulge what Martin was thinking in his mind when he did it. I see that as a betrayal. And I won't do it."

"Does it have anything to do with manipulating me?" I asked, my voice less aggressive.

"No," he said, his eyes steady staring into my own. Jeeves then laid his hand over his heart and leaned toward me, his face relaxing into a soft smile. "I can assure you of that. I promise. It had nothing to do with you. Or Azalea, for that matter."

"Somehow, that doesn't make me feel better."

The vampire's lips pressed with a slight grimace, and his smile wavered as the limo slowed to a stop. "Remember, Fortuna, Martin has other situations here in Mystic's End in addition to the situation with the bottles, besides the one with you. Sometimes it forces him to do things he would prefer not to."

Yeah, that comment didn't make me feel better, either.

FOURTEEN

The limo pulled around toward the back of the compound. I recognized the area—we were near the fence line where Petey had escaped, but everything was dramatically different. The tall chain-link fence separating the undeveloped forest and the greyhound area was newly topped with barbed wire and slatted for privacy. Security cameras on tall poles scanned outward over the clearing like sharks searching for chum.

"You guys work quick," I said. We exited the car to the sound of hammering. "How did all this get done so fast?"

"That gray building over there with the double doors?" Jeeves pointed to a barely visible structure on the other side of the track. "It's construction storage. We have this stuff on hand. Martin just needed to get a work crew out here, so not quite as magical as you would think." He smiled. "You, no doubt, would have been able to get it up much faster."

"Those cameras are new," I observed. "They would have been more useful this morning, don't you think?"

"No doubt why they're up now," Jeeves said, craning his neck toward a scrum of workmen. "There he is."

Jeeves motioned for me to follow, and we walked over toward Martin. He was talking to one of the workmen and pointing west. With a nod, the one turned and shouted to the others. In an instant, they moved the ladders, slats, and tools with swift efficiency.

"I'm glad you're both here." Martin nodded.

"Of course." Jeeves nodded back.

I concentrated, hoping I would hear Jeeves pass Martin information telepathically, but I got nothing. Either Jeeves wasn't talking to Martin, or I could no longer pick up on his directed thoughts.

"No one has seen the dog," Martin told us, his voice low. "I still have at least ten handlers out scouring the forest."

I frowned. "Why are you—"

Jeeves swiftly cut me off. "I'm sure the animal will turn up eventually."

Jeeves hadn't told Martin that Petey was with us. Well, *that* was interesting. With all of Jeeves's declarations of undying loyalty toward Martin, I would have *assumed* he texted him hours ago when he knew.

But he hadn't.

"I hope so," Martin nodded. "I did want to ask you both something. I *distinctly* remember Jeff Abernathy shouting that Ella Grayson had not signed the transfer papers after the dog was already missing. I wanted to check my memory, though, and I recall you two were there. Is that the case?"

"Yeah, I remember." I nodded. "That's why he wanted to call the police, right?"

"My memory is the same as yours and Fortuna's. Why, Martin?"

Martin looked at me, but he said nothing else.

That can't be the reason you called us both back here, Jeeves's voice rang clear in my mind.

Yes! Telepathic spy audio activated.

I wandered toward the fence and pretended to admire the new slats (hoping that my distance and my attention being otherwise occupied would encourage the two further). There was a long silence, and then—

What do you mean, Jeff Abernathy is missing?

Without thinking, I spun around—much to Martin's surprise.

"The reason I asked you is because of this." Martin reached into his back pocket and pulled out papers. Unfolding them, he pulled two sheets apart. "This is an unsigned transfer paper," he said, holding the sheet in his right hand. "This is a signed transfer paper," he added, holding up the sheet in his left. "They're identical in all ways except the filing numbers and names."

"Two different dogs?" I guessed.

"No," Martin shook his head. "This one is for *Bella Bailout X Three Peat Ingathered*. But this one is for a greyhound named *Peter Grayson*."

I frowned. "What about those ear tattoo things? Are those recorded?"

"Tattoo numbers." Martin held up the transfer papers for Bella's racing name. "Microchip number." He held up the documents for Petey. "These papers are for the exact same dog, same markings, same birthday. Two different ways to identify the dog."

"Potentially both valid, too," I murmured. "Do you guys *have* a microchip system?"

"We do, for when the dog leaves the track and gets adopted. We register the dogs with a pet microchip service as a courtesy for adopters," Jeeves explained. "All the kennels have chip guns and chips for that purpose."

"How can we find out if it was activated?"

"I already did," Martin said. "This serial number was activated yesterday evening."

"And no dog's been adopted between then and now?"

Martin shook his head no.

"I don't get it." I frowned. "Pepper found all the insurance policies—"

"For *Bella Bailout X Three Peat Ingathered*." Jeeves pointed out. "Would she or Ollie have even known to look for the other name?"

I didn't know. I didn't know whether they searched for the dog or the people we suspected of being involved in this conspiracy. I pulled out my cell phone and related to Pepper what Martin had just told me, and gave her the microchip number. She promised to have Ollie recheck "the database" with the new information.

I had no idea what database she was talking about, and I didn't ask.

"It's looking more and more like Jeff Abernathy was involved in this somehow," I told Martin after I hung up. "Is he around?" I asked innocently, already knowing darn well he wasn't. "I'd like to talk to him."

"That's the other reason I called you," Martin said, and he gestured toward the gate.

* * *

Hoyt Abernathy sat behind his father's desk as the shuffle and thump of crated greyhounds echoed through the speaker. The whole kennel—dogs, workers, and Hoyt himself—was abnormally quiet.

"Mr. Salvi, sir," Hoyt stood up, his face pale. "No one's heard from him, sir. Hey, Fortuna," he said nervously, nodding toward me. "Daddy's missing. I don't know what to do. But I know something's happened to him. Something *bad*."

"Why do you say that?" I asked.

He jumped up from the desk and ran around, pushing his way through us. Gesturing for us to follow, we went into the main kennel area lined by three levels of relatively large crates. All the cages were filled with beautiful, muscled greyhounds watching us intently. Nervously.

No tails wagged.

"Here." He pointed to a pile of hay on the floor. I squatted down and squinted at the hay, trying to see—

Blood. That's blood.

"I had just laid out fresh hay, not twenty

minutes before I came in here and found it like this."

It was more than the blood, though.

The hay was bunched in piles, and there were footprints in the dirt beneath.

"What did it look like when you left it?" I asked him.

Hoyt leaned against a rough wooden support column and stared down. "It was smooth, like a floor. Daddy always wants the place to look clean, so I change and smooth the hay twice a day. It always has to be even, Pop said. Even and straight in case we get visitors checking out the kennel for their hounds."

I nodded. "And was anyone doing that today?"

Hoyt shrugged. "The initials BR were on Pop's calendar. But I didn't get involved in that stuff."

"Didn't anyone *see* anything?"

"No, ma'am," Hoyt shook his head vigorously. "Daddy told all of us to go in and get a late snack on him. Which was weird, because Pop? Pop isn't the generous sort, if you know what I mean. I should have *known* something was wrong when he told us that. I should have. And now I don't *know* what."

"Okay, so why haven't you called the police?" I said, standing back up. "That's blood. He's missing. A cop might be a good next step, right?"

"So, here's where we're going to sound a little

heartless even though it's the exact opposite of that," Martin told me, shifting uncomfortably. "These papers were filed with the association, by this track. Approved by my secretary. If we call the police and explain all this right now, this track is going to be investigated. This kennel might even get shut down."

"Oh, for goodness sake, Martin, I have no doubt you've greased every palm in this industry from here all the way to England," I told him, rolling my eyes. "Why is *this* suddenly some huge threat to your operation? And why do you care if the kennel gets shut down? Aren't there, like, ten here?"

"It's not a threat to *my* operation," Martin said slowly, staring at me. "Look around you and count the dogs. What happens if this kennel was involved with some kind of fraud?"

"I don't know." I shrugged. "Why don't you tell me."

"If the kennel gets shut down, the dogs have to *go* somewhere. Either to another kennel, or adoption."

"Okay, so far, that sounds great. The dogs get adopted early, another kennel shut down. So, what's the big deal?"

"The big deal is that often there's not a *place* for all of them, and their owners often don't want to pay anything for them to get somewhere even if there is a place," Martin explained slowly—like I was a child having trouble understanding words. "These dogs are *not* beloved pets, Fortuna. They're profit machines. You need to understand the dire situation in the industry right now. There are only eleven tracks left in the country. Florida just outlawed greyhound racing, and tons of tracks will be shutting down in the next month or two. If this kennel shuts down, there is *no doubt* some of these dogs are going to be put down. There won't be enough places for them to go if we have to get rid of them all at once."

"Put down," I said, stunned.

"Yes. Put down."

I glanced around at dog after dog stacked on top of one another as their soft eyes stared back at me. The crates were so small, and the dogs looked so... resigned. "No wonder Gideon came to find me. You would *kill* these dogs just because you didn't want to feed them an extra week or two?"

"*I* don't own the dogs, and *I* don't own the kennel," Martin protested. A greyhound whined.

"No, you own the *track* that makes it all possible. One of only eleven." I glared.

She doesn't understand, Jeeves thought. *Just let it be, Martin.*

"I understand way more than you think,

Sparkles," I snapped. "I think maybe it's you who doesn't understand."

Jeeves stared at me, his eyes surprised. Hoyt looked confused. I tried not to look smug.

"Sparkles?" Hoyt asked, looking back and forth between Jeeves and me.

I rolled my eyes. "Hoyt, tell me absolutely everything you saw, heard—and anything you know about what your father was up to. Let's see if we can figure this out."

I knew that Jeff Abernathy was in the center of whatever conspiracy this was. Maybe he just realized what Ella was up to and took advantage. Perhaps he and Ella concocted this whole plan together.

But either way, I needed more than two pieces of paper as proof—and I needed to get evidence in a way that wouldn't risk the lives of all these innocent dogs.

* * *

At the end of the discussion with Hoyt, I realized one crucial thing.

Hoyt was an idiot.

He had no idea what his father was up to, and no idea where his father could have gone. So many people were angry at Jeff Abernathy that the list of people who could have clocked him on the head and dragged him off was as long as a greyhound's leg.

But...

I kept coming back to the timing. This all happened on the same day Petey ran off, the same day the papers were filed on Petey's two names. The same day Ella Grayson was supposed to ship the dog off to someone in Florida...

As I shuffled through Jeff's paperwork, I found an *incoming* transfer for a greyhound from Florida. The reason for the shipment?

GREYHOUND RACING OUTLAWED, NEW KENNEL NEEDED

"Hey," I looked up from Jeff Abernathy's desk to meet Martin's eyes. "You said Florida just outlawed greyhound racing?"

"Well, a couple of years ago, yes," Martin nodded. "This is the year it's all shutting down."

"So, no more greyhound racing in Florida. At all. Finito, done, over."

"That's right," he said, leaning forward. "I don't think any tracks are operating anymore. Why?"

"If that's true, why would someone buy a *forty-five thousand dollar* racing greyhound and ship it to Florida?"

"I don't know," Martin answered frowning. "That doesn't make any sense. A private owner *wouldn't* pay that much," he said, and then grinned. "Well, except for someone like you. But I find it hard to believe there's anyone like you anywhere. Even in Florida." He winked.

I didn't grin back.

The realization that Martin would have presided over the euthanizing of young, healthy dogs just because they were no longer "profitable" had *almost* made me vomit on his fancy Italian shoes. The idea of *ever* dating him was entirely out of the question now, and the concept of friendship was fading pretty quickly, too.

"Here's who bought Petey," I told Martin. I pulled out a paper and shoved it at him. "Is there some greyhound owner's registry?" He nodded. "Find out who that is. I want to know as much about him as you can uncover."

Martin accepted the paper and stared at me, his smile fading.

She'll get over it, Martin, Jeeves thought to his boss.

"Don't bet on it," I murmured under my breath.

FIFTEEN

"What are you looking at?" Hoyt asked.
I stood in the kennels and gazed at row after row of caged greyhounds. The dogs were all stunning, with bright eyes and sleek hair. They were healthy, at least as far as I could tell. They stared back at me quizzically, as if they didn't understand what I was doing here.

"How long do they stay in those cages? Each day, I mean?"

"We turn 'em out in small groups for an hour or two."

My jaw dropped. "They stay in those small crates for *twenty-two hours a day?*"

Hoyt's feet shuffled awkwardly on the clean floor, He thrust his hands in his pockets. "*Supposed* to. I know what you're thinking, though. That it's not right. Keeping dogs locked up like this." Hoyt appeared thoughtful as he looked at the dogs in his care. They stared back silently.

"Hoyt, that's just one of many, *many* things I'm finding not right about this situation."

He looked at me and gave his head a small shake like he agreed. The resignation on his face told me that even if he agreed, Hoyt had no idea what to do about it. "I try not to care," he mumbled. "It's *hard*, though. I'm with 'em day after day and they...well, they grow on you."

"I don't understand how anyone can approve of this, honestly," I said, turning. "Now that I have a pet greyhound, it astounds me that these animals are kept kenneled for so much of their lives. They must be miserable. I had no idea this racing thing was so...it's just so exploitive. And cruel."

"They're not the only ones miserable," Hoyt said with a sigh.

I looked at him with surprise. "I'm shocked to hear you say what you're saying. Back when I bought Gideon, I wanted to smack you in the face for the way you yanked on him."

"I've never *hurt* a dog," he protested hotly.

I rolled my eyes. "No, you just killed a person."

"You're never gonna let me forget that, are you?"

"Nope," I said quietly.

But something was bothering me.

Hoyt Abernathy struck me as evil when I first met him.

Granted, when I first met him, I discovered he'd hidden Spike's body in my bedroom wall twenty years before as a teenager, and I was doing my best not to invade anyone's psychic privacy. So, I judged him by his deeds with absolutely no real insight into what was going on in his mind.

Standing beside him, though, I sensed something I hadn't expected to. Hoyt Abernathy felt genuine empathy for the hounds in his care, and guilt over the role he played in keeping them imprisoned. That empathy and guilt tugged against the edges of the loyalty and love he had for his father.

"What do *you* think happened to your father?" I asked him.

"I told you. I don't know."

"I'm not asking what you know, Hoyt. I'm asking what you *think*. Even if it's completely out of left field."

After a long pause, Hoyt said, "What I think is he finally pushed someone too far, or got involved in something that finally caught up with him."

Turning from me, he grabbed a rake off the wall and smoothed out the hay so it would be nice and even, the way Jeff Abernathy demanded it always be. "He's been doing things for years that made people mad. Skirted lines. Ripped people off. When Uncle Julius kicked him out of the construction company—"

"I'm sorry," I broke in. "When your uncle did what?"

"Granddad left the construction company to both his sons. My daddy and my Uncle Julius," Hoyt said, stopping to meet my eyes. "My pa borrowed"—Hoyt made air quotes as he said borrowed—"a lot of money from the company. Like, a *lot* of money. Least, that's what Uncle Julius thought. So Uncle Julius threatened to put him in prison for embezzlement if he didn't sign over his half of the company."

"So, your father—"

"Is broke. This is all he has,." Hoyt glanced around the kennel. "And with PeeGrrr and the way things are going with greyhound racing? It ain't much, and it may not be for long."

* * *

When I went back into Jeff Abernathy's office, Martin was gone. However, Jeeves was still sitting behind the desk, typing on the computer.

"So, what'd you find out?" I plopped into a chair.

"Don't you know already?" the vampire responded without halting his quick typing or pulling his eyes away from the screen. "It's clear that you can hear my thoughts."

"That must bug you, huh?" I picked up a stack of papers and thumbed through it.

"It is mildly frustrating, yes."

"Because I can hear you, or because you can't hear me?"

"Yes." The clickety-clack of the keyboard continued without pause. "Did you find out what you wanted to know from Hoyt?"

"I didn't go out there to talk to Hoyt," I said, sighing. "I went out to look at the imprisoned animals in the doggy concentration camp." Jeeves glanced up. "What? That's what it is, isn't it?"

"The dogs at this track are well taken care of. They're fed, kept clean, get good veterinary care—"

"And potentially killed when they outlive their usefulness. *When* is that, by the way?"

He frowned and looked back down at the screen. "When is what?"

"How long do greyhounds race?"

"Most greyhounds are retired between the ages of two and five years."

My jaw dropped. That was barely any time. "And how long do they live?"

"Typically?" Jeeves asked. I nodded. "Between ten and fourteen years."

I swallowed a ball of angry nausea. "And it's *okay* with you that *barely* adult dogs that lived their entire life in a cage might be put down because they didn't run fast enough?"

Jeeves stopped typing and stared at me. "The industry is changing to be far more humane than it once was."

"The industry is getting run out of towns on a rail because it's barbaric," I retorted.

Jeeves looked at me with a mixture of amusement and impatience. "There are some tracks where the dogs are muzzled the entire time they are in their cages—not here. As far as self-regulation, Martin runs one of the more humane tracks with strict care requirements—"

"That's like saying you run the concentration camp that kills the least of any—"

"We're never going to agree on this," Jeeves said, cutting me off. "For one thing, even if I agreed with you, I can't agree with you. I work for Martin, and I work here. Am I happy that profit dictates the care and expendability of these animals at each stage of their development? Of *course* not. Would I prefer that there be no track here? Of course I would. Is there anything *I* can do about it?" He stared at me. "Not at the moment, no. And it's no different than animals being put down in a shelter because they're not adopted."

"Except that these animals worked their whole lives to make someone money, only to risk being discarded like trash when they're not profitable. Why didn't you tell Martin that Petey's with us?" I asked, my eyes narrowing.

"I didn't feel he needed to know."

"Why not?"

Jeeves paused and turned to the computer again, typing swiftly. After twenty seconds, he looked at me, his dark eyes sad. "I can't save them all. I can protect one."

My eyes widened. "From Martin?"

He didn't respond. Once I realized he would not answer, I asked if he had located the buyer in Florida yet. He nodded. "Who is it, then?"

"Jeff Abernathy," Jeeves said, looking up. "The pickup was a ruse. The shipping ticket was counterfeit—no, not even that. The whole company doesn't exist at all. All of this paperwork, the addresses? All fake. If this is to be believed, that dog was never going to leave Mystic's End today."

"Then what was supposed to happen to the dog?" I frowned.

* * *

"Are you accusing me of something?" Martin drew back in surprise at the tone in my voice. "Because if you are, I'd like to know what it is."

"Do I need to accuse you of something?" There was a whole host of things I wanted to accuse him of, to be honest. But I still needed to clear Azalea, find proof against Ella, and now discover what happened to Jeff Abernathy. I didn't have time to give Martin the lecture I wanted to give him over his life choices. "Have you done something nefarious I don't know about?" I rolled my eyes. "Though that's probably a loaded question, isn't it?"

Martin's face flushed red, and I wasn't sure if it was embarrassment or anger. "Fortuna, I—"

"Look, I didn't accuse you of anything," I said, cutting him off. "I just asked if you knew that all of this was fraudulent." With a whoosh, I shoved the pile of papers into Martin's chest.

Struggling to hold the papers in his arms, Martin turned and raised his eyebrow at Jeeves.

It's not a good idea that we speak telepathically around her, Martin. We don't know how much she can pick up.

Oh, for goodness' sake.

I whirled around and glared at Jeeves. "You two are quickly becoming the most untrustworthy people in Mystic's End, you know that? And that's really saying something." The vampire stared back at me, his expression blank. "Why would I bother to help you if I can't trust either one of you? You still need me to bust open those bottles, right?"

"Yes," Martin agreed.

"I would suggest the two of you start opening up a lot more than you have been." I turned back to Martin. "Why did you call the police on Azalea this morning? Jeeves knew she hadn't done it. But you threw her to the wolves, anyway. Why?"

"I—"

"And the truth, Martin. If you ever want me to help you people, I want the *truth*."

"The truth is that I am a prominent business owner in this town, and your assistant wasn't worth risking my relationship with Chief Clutterbuck. That's the truth," Martin told me while placing the sheaf of papers back down on Jeff Abernathy's desk. "You are not my only concern, as much as I might wish you were. Evangeline was already plugged in to what was going on here, and Clutterbuck would have known Azalea turned up if I didn't call him."

"The only thing Evangeline Laroux is plugged in to is a whiskey bottle." I shot him a fierce look.

"Gabe investigated me repeatedly. Unlike my father, I follow the law to the best of my ability, Fortuna. And considering my father, that's not always easy." Martin stared at me intently, as if his seriousness would make me understand his point by force of will alone. "I was asked to call, and I did."

"That would be a much more believable story if you had called the police about the pool of blood in the kennel." I realized that Martin had his own criteria regarding what laws to follow, and what right and wrong applied to him.

"I told you why I haven't called them," Martin responded, a surprised look on his face. "I thought you'd understand that reasoning, at least. I don't want to put the dogs' lives in jeopardy."

"The dogs' lives are in jeopardy because of what you *do* for a living, Martin," I told him angrily, the lecture spilling out of me. "You opened a greyhound track. You built this monstrosity around that track with the casinos and restaurants and hotel and club. All of this only exists because of you and your money. Everything that's happening here can be traced back to you, ultimately. You made all these things possible. This is what you built."

He scraped his hand through his hair and shifted on his feet. "I do more than most—"

"And yet PeeGrrr thinks that's maybe not enough."

"I don't care what they think. I care what you think."

I crossed my arms. "I think it's definitely not enough."

Martin was tense, his muscles twitching as he stared at me.

I didn't like the turn our relationship had taken —but there were things he did that I just couldn't ignore anymore. Martin could claim he was trying to be a good person, claim he was trying to legitimize his mafia family's business, and claim he cared about doing the right thing.

Those claims, though, got very wobbly upon closer inspection—and his choice to wrap himself in psychic protections so I could barely read him meant that I *didn't* know if malice roiled beneath his calm exterior. Maybe judging him solely by his actions, like with Hoyt, was making me jump to the wrong conclusions. But what choice was he giving me?

Martin reached out for me tentatively, slowly... and then changed his mind. "Look, I need you," he confessed.

"So?"

His face cracked, and his bravado slipped just a little. "This isn't you, Fortuna. I know you're angry, but this isn't you. Maybe we should take some time for you to calm down, and think about—"

"Maybe you don't know me very well, Martin," I cut him off. "I may have only been turned into a full witch in the last year, but I've been a telepath all my life. I learned very, very early on that everything has an energy, a spirit. I can't even step on a bug without feeling horrible about myself. You?" I let out a breath and leaned back against the desk. "You imprison dogs. You admit that you would have overseen a potential mass culling of dogs because of mistakes the humans around them made. You shrug off these beings as profit-making automatons as opposed to fully-realized sentient, breathing, living things."

Martin swallowed hard. "Fortuna, I—"

"Stop. Just stop. It isn't surprising," I told him. "I don't know why I am surprised. I shouldn't be. Your family has been running an indentured paranormal servant racket for who knows how long." I glanced at Jeeves. The vampire stood about two feet away from Martin, a distressed look on his face. "You can talk to people's faces and still bend them to your will. Willingly, not willingly? I don't know. You've only let me meet him." I pointed.

"Martin has to be careful, Fortuna," Jeeves said. "Jerome Watson, Martin's butler, reports everything we do here back to Martin's father. Marty Salvatore is a dangerous man," the vampire warned. "You don't understand the situation that Martin is in."

"Of course not," I responded. "You only share with me what you want me to know."

"That's for your protection," Martin insisted.

I held out my hand and created a ball of seething, pulsing energy, one of the first things Gunther ever taught me how to do. It wasn't a weapon; it was nothing more than a child witch's first steps toward trying to tap into the energy all around us.

But it *looked* super scary.

"I can take care of myself," I said as the energy buzzed.

Someone shouted, "What the hell!" It was followed by the sound of something heavy crashing in the doorway, and I turned to find Hoyt Abernathy passed out on the floor.

SIXTEEN

The benefits of knowing a vampire? He can take something directly out of a human's mind. He (or she) can also manipulate a memory, so it fits a different narrative. They can even make a target human comfortable with what they know or see, so they never give it a second thought.

At least I think so. Jeeves never confirmed it, but that's what some vampire books claimed.

While ushering me out, Jeeves promised to make sure Hoyt didn't recall I was ever in the office —much less that I stood there holding a sparkling, glowing energy ball in my palm.

Once the dude came to, anyway.

"I will head over to your shop once I deal with the human," Jeeves told me before I left.

I don't know how he knew I had to get the heck out of there, but I did. I had an overwhelming desire to put as much distance between me and the track as I could, I was so disgusted with it all. The stone was still firmly against my skin blocking his ability to read me. He *shouldn't* have been able to telepathically pick up on anything.

Maybe he was getting to know me.

Maybe, since we spent so much time together, he was able to just...know.

As I stepped out of the limo in front of my shop, I glanced across the street to find the make-upped guy in leather slipping out of the old courthouse building once again.

Huh.

I watched him angle through the courtyard and slip around to the west side parking spaces. He jumped quickly into the driver's seat of a large white van. No windows. Without looking around, he backed up and drove away toward the setting sun.

"What is he doing?" I murmured, watching the van driving away.

"What's who doing?" called a voice from behind me. I turned to find Pepper walking out of my shop.

"What are you doing here?" I asked Pepper. "I thought you were going to the wake with Claire."

"I did." She stepped up beside me. "Claire was so messed up she couldn't stay long. What are you looking at?" Pepper frowned. "That's a lot of *whats* in one conversation."

"There's this guy I've seen *twice* now," I pointed. "He's going in and out of the old courthouse building. Gabe mentioned there's really not much in there anymore. The thing is, he doesn't look like someone that would be going in and out of a records building."

"Well, that's judgmental." Pepper craned her head around looking for him. "Which guy?"

"He left just before you came out here. In a white, windowless van."

"Well, that's not creepy at all."

"I know, right?"

Help me.

I froze and listened.

"What's wrong?" Pepper asked me, frowning.

"I heard something."

"I didn't hear anything."

"No, not with my ears," I said distractedly, straining to pick up more. I waited ten, twenty, thirty seconds. Nothing. "Come on, dude." Standing on the sidewalk in the twilight, I whispered to the air around me. "I need more than that." The center of Mystic's End was soundless except for the occasional car driving by. Frowning, I shrugged. "Maybe I just thought I heard something."

But I couldn't shake the unsettling feeling I was missing something right in front of me.

* * *

"So, what did you find out at the track?" Pepper asked once we were inside.

"That greyhound racing is a lot crueler than I thought it was when I came here." My friend caught my eye as we sat down on the couches and raised a questioning eyebrow. "Well, I mean, I knew that Gideon was unhappy there, but he was healthy and not abused, so—"

"Let me guess," Pepper said, cutting me off. "You've discovered how many dogs they 'cull.'" As she said *cull*, she made air quotes. "Racing greyhounds have three states of being. Healthy, injured, and dead. And even healthy, it's *not* much of a life."

"I didn't even know they 'culled' dogs at all." I wrapped my hands around myself and shuddered. "Martin made it sound like they run, and then they get adopted. He never mentioned the possibility of animals getting euthanized until today. In fact, he *implied* that his family used magic to keep that kind of thing from happening here."

"At every stage, those dogs are at risk." Pepper nodded. "Too small in the litter? Culled. Ran your first race and you suck? Culled. The owner doesn't want to pay to have a dog transferred? Culled. The dog got injured running a race? Culled. Now, it's better than it *used* to be, don't get me wrong," she said, waving her hands animatedly. "It's not a death camp."

I decided not to argue about my disagreement.

"And Martin does put a lot of money into finding as many of the dogs homes as possible, and setting pretty strict kennel rules about euthanizing dogs. He organizes regular adoption days and covers boarding fees. But is that a no-kill greyhound track?" she asked me. "No. Not by a long shot. How'd you find out?"

"Jeff Abernathy is missing," I told Pepper, and then explained what I'd learned that afternoon at the track. "When I asked Martin why he hadn't called the police, he said that the greyhound association or government or someone would investigate. If the kennel had to shut down, some of the dogs would possibly be put down because they'd have nowhere to go. So he didn't call."

Gideon watched me from his pillow. His dark, soulful eyes stared intently at me.

"Well, that's kind of him, at least. Though not, I guess, if you're Jeff Abernathy."

"If he didn't perpetuate a sport that caused the death of his athletes for money, maybe he wouldn't have to make decisions like that," I responded harshly.

"Whoa." Pepper blinked. "You really *didn't* know, did you?"

"I mean, I knew the track wasn't..." I trailed off and sat silently, uncomfortable with the real source of my anger. Because the real cause of my anger was me.

The fact is, I never looked into it. I got attached to Gideon, I bought him, and I considered that act good enough. I didn't find out what happened to him before me, or what could have happened to him had I not taken him home. I expressed my displeasure at Martin regarding what he did (over a ridiculously fancy dinner *he* bought), but that was it. "No, I didn't know the extent of it," I said finally. "I didn't look into it. And since I was thinking about dating Martin, I should have."

"Well, you know now. What are you going to do?"

I didn't know.

But one thing I *did* know.

Martin and I would not be dating until

greyhound racing was shut down, and *every* dog at that track had a home.

And perhaps not even then.

* * *

Gabe escorted Miss Bessie into the store as Pepper rolled her eyes.

"I *saw* that, Miss Thing," Miss Bessie snapped. She shrugged off Gabe's guiding hand. "I'm sure I have you to thank for losing Gabe his job!"

"I'm sure you don't, Miss Bessie," she responded, pointing at me. "You may want to thank your protégé over there. I'm pretty sure Gabe getting fired was more or less her fault. Blame her." Pepper smirked at me. I glared back at her.

"Fortuna, I knew you were magic," Miss Bessie gushed as she shuffled over and leaned in to give me a quick hug. "I've wanted Gabriel to get out of that cesspool for years!"

"Hey, wait a minute!" Pepper raced over and placed a hand on Miss Bessie's back. "If I'd known you were *happy* about it, I totally would have taken the credit! I had a lot to do with it—"

"Too late," the old woman snapped.

Gabe stood in the center of the room, his brow knit in a pained expression. "Gram, this isn't something to celebrate. I lost my pension, my insurance. I have some savings, I'll be able to handle the home for a few months, but I don't know what I'm going to do. My degree isn't—"

"You are faithful, conscientious, and a good man to a fault, Gabriel Wilcox," Miss Bessie told him, her eyes moist. "That department was blackening your soul, holding you back from your full potential. It was never a place for the noble-minded. I think you know that." She shuffled over to him and looked up into his eyes. "Your moral constitution will be much happier with what you do next."

"But Gram," he said softly. "I don't *know* what to do next."

"You are the son of witch blood, and the grandson of the former mystic of this town, child," Miss Bessie told him, her eyes twinkling with excitement. "Nobility runs through your very DNA. Now, you can—"

"Hold on there, Gram," Gabe said, stepping back from her and staring down in surprise. "What do you mean, witch blood?" He glanced at me, his face a tense expression of concern. "What is she talking about?" Looking back down at her, he repeated the question. "What are you talking about?"

Pepper was uncharacteristically silent.

Gideon walked over to Gabe and pressed himself against Gabe's leg.

The tension in the room was profound. I thought it was because Miss Bessie was about to tell Gabe everything she had hidden from him all his life. About her. About his mother. About the witch bottles. And I was right. She was.

I was also wrong.

So wrong.

"All my life, I've protected you from the truth of who your momma was. Who *I* was. The history of our family in this town," Miss Bessie told him breathlessly. Her typically harsh voice was almost soft as she opened up to her grandson about their magical heritage for the first time. "I didn't want you to get hurt, Gabriel. My angel boy." The old woman's eyes teared up. "But now you're free. You're free to be who I always knew you could be."

"Could you stop talking like we're in one of your Hallmark movies and just *tell* me what you mean?" Gabe asked her gently but insistently.

"Gabe." Pepper moved toward him, but his eyes cut to her, and his face looked fierce.

"Don't. Just *don't*."

Pepper stopped.

Miss Bessie was an expert manipulator, but I could sense no guile from her. All I could sense was peace, joy, and happiness. As if something that she waited for had finally come to pass. As if her...

As if her job...

...was done.

"Oh, no, ma'am," I told her. I felt the flood of relief she was spraying in every direction. The excitement she could relieve Gabe's burden. Enthusiasm for all the new things she could do. I stepped up and pointed my finger at her. "Don't you even think about—"

"You hush," she admonished me. "I know what I need to do."

"Miss Bessie, don't you dare!" I shouted. My insides were twisting in fear.

She wouldn't.

She couldn't.

"What the hell is going on here?" Gabe asked, his voice brimming over with frustration. He looked down at his grandmother and took her in his arms. "Gram, what is all this? What are you talking about?" Looking into her watery blue eyes, he saw something that frightened him. "Gram, please, tell me what's going on," he whispered.

"I will, dear boy," she smiled and kissed him. Her bony hand caressed his face. "I will. Or Fortuna will. We'll have all the time in the world. It'll all be okay. I promise you. We'll talk soon."

With a last gasp, Miss Bessie collapsed in Gabe's arms.

And died.

* * *

"This isn't happening," I whispered, watching the paramedics load Miss Bessie onto the stretcher. "This isn't happening. I can't believe this is happening."

Gabe was inconsolable as silent cries wracked his body. Pepper wrapped an arm about his waist and was trying to comfort him, her eyes filled with tears. The EMTs gently pushed him aside, but seeing their frustratingly slow movements as they attempted to save Miss Bessie's life, my heart sank. Their actions made it clear neither of them expected her to open her eyes ever again.

Which would be right. In one sense.

In another, so very, very wrong.

"Oh, my lord, I feel so *wonderful!*" Miss Bessie's ghost twirled around my storefront. "No more arthritis, no more bursitis, no more *heartburn!* No more aches and pains!" The old woman stared at me. "Watch!" With a snap of her spectral fingers, Miss Bessie dropped a hundred pounds and two hundred wrinkles. "I *told* you I was a looker back in the day.

This isn't even that far back in the day, Fortuna. I've grown fond of my white hair, you know. Oh, watch this!" She snapped her fingers again. "You like this dress? I haven't worn red in years."

I stared at her in horror. "This isn't happening."

"I was *old*, sweet cheeks," the ghost cackled at me. She looked down and admired her new body. "Did you think I was going to wait at that old folks home forever? No, as soon as Gabriel shook himself free from that police department, I *knew* it was time. He's got to find his own way without being concerned about paying for my room. Besides, there's a waiting list a mile long to get into the place. I'm sure someone will take the room."

"This isn't about your room at the old folks' home!" I whispered at her. Pepper's head snapped up, and her eyes narrowed. "How could you do that to Gabe?"

"Gabe will be fine," Miss Bessie chided me. "You'll tell him to load that app on his fancy phone, and I'll be able to talk to him. What's more important, though, is that I'll be able to help you. *All* the time." Miss Bessie smiled mischievously. "I'll never be far. Just think of the things we'll be able to do together! Aren't you excited?"

I was not excited. "This. Isn't. Happening."

"Stop repeating yourself, dear. You sound like a broken record." Miss Bessie ricocheted around the storefront, snapping through a variety of outfits as Gideon barked and chased her happily. She seemed euphoric. "Tell Gabe I'm here so he can stop being all mopey."

Pepper was still staring at me, her eyes shining with curiosity. Gabe moved to follow the paramedics out the door when I shook my head to her. She nodded and turned. "Hey, let's take the car, Gabe," Pepper suggested gently, holding him back. He was so devastated he just slumped, allowing himself to be led back in the store.

"It was like she knew," Gabe whispered in a ragged voice. The ambulance turned on its lights and bathed the room in blue and red, but no siren wail pierced the quiet of the evening as they pulled away. "She looked me in the eyes, and I swear, Fortuna—she *knew*."

"I know she did, Gabe." I swallowed. "And I know because she's here."

"Well, of course, she'll always be here," he responded brokenly. "I'll carry her in my heart forever."

"Um, I don't think you understand me." I shook my head. "I mean she's *here*. Miss Bessie *decided* she wanted to be a ghost, left her body, and now she's here flitting around my store talking up a storm."

Pepper dropped her arms and stared at me, her

face white. "Oh, holy sh—" she started, but Gabe cut her off.

"Wait a minute. Just wait a minute. Wait."

"I'm waiting," I answered.

He pulled himself up to his full height and stared. "What are you saying? Exactly?"

"I don't think I can make it any clearer than that, Gabe," I responded. "Your grandmother's not gone. She's here, she just...changed form, I guess."

He looked around the room frantically—the way he did when I first told him about Spike.

"Gabe, you can't see her."

He waved his arms in the air.

"Oh, he looks ridiculous. Tell him that I'm fine, and not to be sad. I feel better than I have in years," Miss Bessie demanded.

So I did.

"You're just saying this to make me feel better," Gabe accused. He dropped his arms, tears welling up in his eyes again.

"You tell him that when he was five years old, he peed all over the sunflowers because he thought his pee would help make them more yellow," Miss Bessie said, crossing her arms. "You tell him. No one knows about that but us."

So I did.

Gabe's face burned hot. "Okay, okay, I believe you." His head twisted on his neck as he continued to look around. I don't know what he was hoping to glimpse, but I was sure he would never see it.

"What are you looking for?"

Gabe stopped and turned toward me, his eyes hopeful. "Is Mom here? Did she come to meet her?" he asked, a catch in his throat. The longing that poured off him was enough to break anyone's heart, but I had to tell him she wasn't.

"Tell him why," Miss Bessie demanded. "It's time for him to know the whole story."

So I did.

SEVENTEEN

The whole story—that Gabe's mother's soul was *probably* trapped in a witch bottle, Miss Bessie had been a powerful witch called the mystic, and that she'd passed that title and power on to me—wasn't easy for Gabe to hear. Miss Bessie knew it wouldn't be, too—right before I laid it out for him, Miss Bessie wondered out loud if Gabe would be as angry as she suspected he would be.

He was as angry as she suspected he would be.

So angry that at the end of the tale (and asking no questions), he stormed out, Pepper on his heels.

"Well, I'm glad I waited to tell him until after I was dead, then, if he's going to act like a petulant child," Miss Bessie said with a shrug. "I guess I made the right decision. That's a fight I don't have to have, right? He's going to be a pain for you to deal with for a while."

"You didn't wait to tell him. You made *me* tell him. And not for nothing, but is that really what you got out of what just happened?" I asked her with a raised brow, shocked at her lack of sympathy for poor Gabe. Even Gideon was staring at the ghost as if he couldn't quite believe her attitude. "He feels utterly betrayed by you, Miss Bessie. And he's just had the second worse twenty-four hours of his life—he lost his job *and* the only family he has left all on the same day."

"He didn't *lose* me, dear. I'm right here!" The ghost smiled brightly at me and twirled away. Gideon tilted his head and made his confused sound. The one that sounded suspiciously like "Huh?"

New ghosts can be terrified by what's happening to them. If they're not prepared, if they have preconceived notions of what death will be like? They *can* be frozen with fear. It can take them a bit—could be a day or hundreds of years—to get their head together and adjust to their new reality.

Prepared ghosts, dead people that knew what they were moving into? They have their own challenges. They can be a little punch drunk with their newfound spirit-only existence and all the freedom that entails.

Miss Bessie? She was punch drunk.

And not thinking clearly.

"Look, again—*you* didn't tell him any of this." I crossed my arms and frowned, watching the older woman admire herself. "As far as *he's* concerned, he just lost you. Since he also just lost his career to boot, you really picked a heck of a time to do this. In the middle of that trauma, he just gained a lot of knowledge about his family that you did *nothing* to prepare him for."

Help me.

My head snapped up, and I listened.

"Fortuna, you're bumming me out." Miss Bessie floated toward me. "It's *my* death day, you should—"

"Be quiet!" I hissed, holding up my hand. "I heard something."

"I didn't hear anything." Miss Bessie stopped gallivanting and listened. "Nope, not a thing."

"That's good, that means whoever's calling for help isn't dead," I murmured.

"Someone's calling for help?"

"It's the second time I heard it." I walked toward the front door and stepped out. Scanning the quiet, dark street, nothing seemed out of place. Cocking my head to the side, I concentrated as Miss

Bessie flew through the window. She floated directly in front of me and stared.

"Just forget about it and come back inside! We have a lot of work to do! We need to start looking for the bottles, we need to check the book, we need to go—"

"*Stop* talking," I said, sidestepping her and continuing to scan the quiet street.

Miss Bessie squinted and gave me a hard smile. "I don't have to. You can't do anything to me now, I'm a ghost."

"I'll tell you what I told Spike. I can banish you from my building," I told her, hitching my thumb toward my shop. "And I can seal it up so I can't hear you haranguing me outside. You can fly in circles around it complaining until the cows come home, and it won't bother me a bit. So just be quiet for a minute so I can listen."

As I watched, the mysterious white van pulled up. This time, two people got out—the leather-clad man, and Zach Johnson. I jumped back into my doorway and hoped they couldn't see me. With a quick glance around, they headed inside the old courthouse.

"Come on," I whispered, and headed across the street.

* * *

"What are we doing here?" Miss Bessie asked, floating behind me. I shrugged and pointed toward the stairway. Heavy footsteps echoed from below, and shadows flickered in the low-lit hallway below. "You know, if you're going to follow two men into the bowels of an old building at night, you should at least dim your shine, there, girl."

I turned and held up my hands silently, raising an eyebrow.

"Dim your shine! Dim your shine! You know, cast a spell so that you're harder to see!"

That would be great, I agree. If I knew how to do that.

I clasped my hands under my chin in a gesture of prayer, and then jerked my head toward Miss Bessie.

"You want me to tell you how? Now? Don't you think you should have learned this before we were alone down here in the middle of the night?"

I dropped my hands and glared.

"Oh, all right," Miss Bessie harrumphed. "Just whisper *Corium* and cross your first and second fingers on both your hands. No, your thumb and pointy finger." The ghost showed me, holding up her hands. "Yes. That's it. Now whisper the word. It will make you hard to see, but not invisible, so you still need to be careful."

I looked at my wrist and tapped it as if there was a watch there.

Miss Bessie looked confused for a minute and then nodded once she understood. "Twenty minutes, maybe slightly more," she told me, her voice lowering even though the two men down below couldn't hear her. "You're not carrying anything that would make noise, are you? It won't work on that. Just you."

I patted myself to make sure I didn't have my phone, but I did. Stepping quickly outside the courthouse door, I placed my phone on the sidewalk just outside. Scurrying back in, I held up my hands as if to ask if there was anything further.

"Nope, just cross your fingers and whisper the word."

I did, and Miss Bessie nodded. Then we stood there looking at each other.

"Well?" she asked me. "You just going to stand there while time ticks away?"

I buried my head in my hands and counted to ten, sighing. When I looked up, I pointed to her, pointed down the stairs, pointed to me, and then pointed down the stairs.

"You want me to go first? I'm an old woman, Fortuna!" As Miss Bessie protested about her feebleness, I marched through her once, twice, and again. Just to make sure that she remembered she was dead, and I was not. Her death made her the ideal person to scout ahead.

"Oh, right." Miss Bessie glanced down the stairs. "I should probably go first and let you know if it's safe, right? They can't see or hear me." She gave a self-deprecating laugh and cleared her throat. "Well, that was embarrassing. Shall we?"

I extended my arm out as if she was a movie star, and the stairs were a red carpet.

* * *

The steps lead to a dingy, damp hallway. There were no decorations on the walls, no chairs. The reinforced steel doors on either side of the corridor gave it a prison-like feel.

"You know, they built this in 1888?" Miss Bessie said as we crept along the passageway. "Only cost $25,000 back then. Can you imagine? This whole building for half the money you paid for your dog."

It made sense. The building was a substantial stone structure, and the lack of ventilation in this part of the building made it feel like a dungeon. It would have been easy to surmise this old place was haunted, but I saw no ghosts other than the old woman I followed.

It was clear from the layer of dust covering

everything that few people ventured into this part of the old courthouse, and I struggled not to sneeze. No signs were denoting where the doors lead, and hardly any lights. If Miss Bessie didn't possess an otherworldly glow, I would have had to grope my way through.

"There's a light up ahead," Miss Bessie whispered. "Stay close."

We came upon another hall, and the men's voices became louder. I stopped just before the corner and motioned for her to look. She nodded while I stayed well hidden—I didn't know how hard I was to see, but there seemed to be no reason to take any unnecessary chances.

"Tell us where the dog is!" a gruff voice I didn't recognize shouted.

"I don't know, I don't know," a quiet voice moaned. I could barely understand the man, he sounded so muffled—as if his mouth was filled with marbles. "Please, just let me go. I didn't do anything."

"You've done plenty," Zach Johnson said immediately, his voice guttural. The sound of a loud clang, a groan, and then panting "For years, you've made money off animals, and you weren't even grateful to them. You treated them like dogs!"

"They *are* dogs, you idiots," the voice protested with contempt. I recognized it now.

It was Jeff Abernathy.

"You don't know when to shut up, do you?" the other voice said. Another loud clang, another moan, and I suddenly gasped as I picked up on Jeff Abernathy's intense fear. Pain, and a wave of almost drunken nausea. I couldn't tell whether it was from his injuries, or he'd been drugged.

I sniffed and rubbed my nose, itchy from all the dust.

Sudden silence.

Oops.

"Did you hear that?" the unidentified man asked.

"I didn't hear anything except this coward," Zach responded.

I stepped backward and hid in a doorway, closed my eyes, and tried to telepathically place myself in Jeff Abernathy's shoes.

* * *

He wasn't hurt.

Well, he wasn't *severely* hurt.

Jeff's face throbbed around his nose area, but he was otherwise unharmed. He seemed to be in an old-fashioned jail cell, and I suddenly remembered Gabe's description of this building. Though he neglected to mention the sheer creep factor of this place.

The kennel owner's captors had leashed him and tied the leash to one of the metal beds welded to the cage-like bars. His face was...contained somehow. I could feel it was difficult for him to breathe, to talk—as if something was wrapped around his face.

"I don't know what you want from me," Jeff implored the two men.

"I want to know where the dog is," Zach told him fiercely, gripping a metal baton in his hand.

Well. That explained the clang.

"I want to know what plan you and Ella concocted to murder my sister!" the other man shouted. "Tell me what the two of you did or you're *never leaving this basement!*"

BR

Brock. Brock Grayson.

The man in the leather was Brock Grayson, Bella Grayson's fraternal twin brother. And he seemed convinced, totally convinced, that Jeff Abernathy and Ella Grayson plotted together to murder his sister.

"I didn't do nothing," Jeff mumbled, and then reached up to tug on the thing that wrapped around his face. It felt like leather, with holes in it. I realized he was effectively muzzled. "I'm just a kennel owner. I didn't do anything."

He was *muzzled.*

Like a track greyhound.

"I *know* you did something," Brock seethed at the man. "I found the bottle of fentanyl in my sister's things. A bottle from *your* track, Abernathy. With *your* kennel's control stamp on it. How would Ella have got a bottle of dog sedatives from the locked med area you showed me today? Huh? And why would she yank it from my hand and destroy it, huh?"

"I didn't show you anything," Abernathy mumbled. "Maybe your sister was a druggie. Maybe she stole it."

"I have you on video!" he said, pulling a camera from his pocket. "I have the bottles on video! I know that the control number is from your cabinet, Abernathy, and I know you had the only key! The bottle I found in Bella's house had *your* control number. Now stop making excuses and tell me what you and Ella did! Tell me why you killed my sister!"

"Oh, shut the hell up! You don't have evidence of nothin'," Jeff Abernathy told him, a menacing threat creeping into his voice. "You don't have nothin'. Ella took that bottle from you, and I suspect it's long gone by now. If you did have it, you wouldn't have kidnapped me. You woulda called the police. Now, when this is all over, *you'll* go to jail. Not me."

"Uh oh, Brock, he may be right. They *do* put people in prison for murder. That is, they do *if* they can find a body," Zach said to Bella's brother. His casual offhandedness *was* chilling—but I could sense that neither man was capable of murder.

Angry, yes. Furious, even. And yes, they both desperately *wished* they were capable of ending Jeff Abernathy right in the old jail cell.

But I could feel neither of them had it in them.

I dug around in Jeff Abernathy's mind trying to find some bit of evidence he may have left, but despite his bravado, he was scared. He was *so* emotionally overwhelmed by the situation he was in that I could get nothing specific to grab on to. Papers kept flashing in his mind like a warning, but just as I tried to determine what it was, fear overtook his entire being. It slipped away, drowned out by the panic he was trying to hide.

Jeff was far less confident in his ability to escape this than he pretended to be when facing his captors.

I, on the other hand, was confident he would just be scared and uncomfortable for a while. I slipped back into my own mind and made my way silently toward the building's entrance. I struggled not to take any smug glee in the fact that Jeff Abernathy likely felt the way the greyhounds at his kennel felt.

That was, no doubt, Zach and Brock's intention.

EIGHTEEN

"Looking for this?"

I squinted toward the voice and spotted Jeeves. He stood on the sidewalk and held out the cell phone I had been searching for in the bushes near the old courthouse's main entrance.

"If you got the cell phone before I came out here, why did you stand there and watch me paw through the flora for three solid minutes?" I asked with exasperation.

Jeeves moved toward me with his hand extended but paused halfway. He tilted his head as if contemplating whether to answer me truthfully. Or, knowing him, whether to answer me at all. "Truthfully?"

"No. Lie to me, Sparkles. Let's keep this entertaining," I said when I reached him and snatched it out of his hand. Our fingers grazed one another briefly as I yanked, and his skin felt surprisingly warm.

I hoped he hadn't drunk anyone on the way over.

"I wanted to see if you would use magic to find it," he told me, his eyes sparkling with amusement. Turning, he bowed slightly. "Miss Bessie. Let me be the first to welcome you to the tribe of the dead. I hope your death was nothing painful."

"Well, don't *you* look different," she squinted, tilting her head. "I didn't know a vampire could be paler than a ghost, but you are just a walking alabaster statue, aren't ya?"

Jeeves lifted his eyebrows briefly but said nothing. The ghost and the vampire stared at one another as if engaging in a silent conversation that I, being alive, couldn't participate in. Finally, Miss Bessie turned while muttering something I couldn't hear and moved away.

Weird.

"So, we found Jeff Abernathy," I said to break the silence. "He's—"

"I know," Jeeves interrupted politely. "I heard most of what you overheard as well." Tapping his ears, Jeeves smiled briefly. "Super hearing, remember?"

"The problem is if Zach and Brock are right, we *still* don't really have any proof of anything to take to Detective Conroe. Not to clear Azalea or implicate Ella as Bella's murderer. It's all circumstantial."

"I think there's a clear—"

"I don't know." I exhaled and leaned against a lamppost. "He's so incredibly freaked out that his mind was a jumble of indignation that they were doing this to him, *and* fear that he'd wind up stuffed in a wall, like Spike. It's hard to pick psychic leaves out of a mental tornado."

"Do you think he would turn on Ella to save his own skin?"

"I think Jeff Abernathy would turn on anyone to save his own skin," I answered truthfully.

"We need clear-cut evidence that Ella injected Bella with the fentanyl, or we'll need to persuade Jeff Abernathy to turn on his co-conspirator." Jeeves tilted his head. "I just had a thought. The men below said that Ella had taken or thrown away or destroyed the bottle of fentanyl with the control number on it, correct?"

I nodded.

"Your friend Ollie said there was a massive amount of the drug in the girl. The fentanyl at the track is used for..." Pausing, Jeeves shifted uncomfortably as his eyes glanced away from mine. After a moment, he turned back. "Well, in any case, it's an *injectable* form. There must have been a syringe," Jeeves said.

"Oh, come on. Ella wouldn't be *that* stupid, would she? Keeping that around?"

"Ella kept the bottle of the drug around long enough for Brock Grayson to fly back into the country, go to the home she shares with her deceased wife, *and* look around to find the bottle. She also did all this without even confirming *for sure* that she was married and would inherit the fortune. That was, no doubt, the reason she did all this in the first place—considering her behavior." Jeeves shrugged. "It doesn't sound to me like she's all that meticulous a criminal."

"Unlike you and Martin," I said curtly.

His slight smile remained, but I could sense a subtle shift in attitude at my reminder of what he did for a living—and the reminder of how I felt about it. "We all have our skills," he said softly, a hint of steel beneath his gentle tone.

* * *

The house of Bella and Ella Grayson was quiet as we slipped in. Miss Bessie and Jeeves, together, were proving to be useful to have around. Miss Bessie scouted the place before we broke in and pronounced it empty, while Jeeves listened for approaching cars.

Okay, I wasn't too shabby, either, to be honest. Apparently, picking locks involved a finger wiggle and the whisper of the word *patefio*.

"I remember reading she was found in the big bedroom upstairs," I told Jeeves quietly, and headed for the stairs. He nodded once and followed. Miss Bessie simply went upwards and disappeared into the white ceiling. "Okay, I could see how that would be useful," I murmured.

"You don't seem to be angry at her," Jeeves observed from behind.

"Not everything is as it appears, Sparkles."

"That's good," he replied.

I stopped on the stairway and stared at him. "Good? Why would that be good?"

He looked up at me with a half-smile. "I thought it was just mine and Martin's life choices you passed judgment on. Since that's not the case, I feel a bit better."

"I'm not passing judgment on anyone's life choices!" I protested hotly, my hands planted on my hips. I jutted my jaw out in defiance...and then realized I looked kind of judgmental—just a little. Dropping my hands, I sighed. "Look, maybe I am.

But I have a problem with people that do things that hurt other people."

He smiled up at me, his head tilted. "Who have I hurt?"

My jaw dropped. "Anyone you've slurped up like a salty iron-flavored milkshake, maybe?"

"Are you two going to jibber-jabber on those steps all night?" Miss Bessie screeched from above. "I think I found something up here!"

Jeeves stepped up.

The vampire must have taken the step with the assumption I would turn and rush up the stairs to answer Miss Bessie's implied demand, but I didn't. I delayed a few seconds.

Just long enough for the vampire to take that step.

Just one step.

That one step put him face to face with me.

Jeeves's nose was suddenly just inches from my own, his intense eyes so close I could mark the flecks of amber in them—even in the dark. The pressure of his body, his hand so close to mine on the banister suddenly felt intimate. My breath caught in my chest as I breathed him in. I realized his skin seemed to carry the delicate scent of sandalwood.

"Fortuna," Jeeves said, his voice suddenly husky.

"Uh huh," I sighed, nodding, and staring into his eyes.

"This stairway is too narrow for me to move around you," he told me.

"Uh huh," I answered again, breathlessly.

I seemed to lose the capacity for words.

And thoughts.

And movement.

All at the same time.

I struggled to pull myself out of his spell. Reminded myself that Jeeves was a vampire, and vampires were powerfully attractive to humans. It was the same way people desperately wished to pet a tiger even though they knew the tiger could tear them limb from limb. Sure, I was a witch, but apparently, I was still human enough not to be immune to his powerful magnetism.

That's all it was, I told myself. I turned away and raced up the stairs.

He was just a vampire.

It meant nothing.

* * *

"There," Miss Bessie pointed as I walked in. As she glanced up, her eyes narrowed, and the ghost gave me a sharp look. "Busy, were we?" Her tone was loaded with accusations.

"We were just talking," I told her, though my hands rubbed together as if they were trying to wipe away the memory of the vampire's touch. "What did you find?"

"I'm pointing at it, girl." The old woman snapped and jerked her pointed finger toward the corner again. "Snap out of it and get back in the game, will you? I want to get this over and done with, so we can start looking for the witch bottles. These little side trips of yours take too long."

"Weren't *you* the one that told me it's the mystic's job to protect the town?"

"Did I say that?" Miss Bessie asked innocently, but she didn't deny it.

The bathroom was small but colorful. A dented toothpaste tube sat on the glazed sink, the cap off. A black toothbrush lay next to it—while a white one peeked out of the wastebasket. "Where?"

"Behind the trash." Jeeves carefully moved the small can. "There, do you see that bag? The needle peaking out of it?" His eyes went soft, and he sniffed. "There's blood in there."

Suddenly, a door slammed from below, and I looked up, my eyes wide.

"I'll go see who it is," Miss Bessie announced, and she floated out through the wall.

"What do we—"

That's all I got out of my mouth before Jeeves

grabbed me and leaped across the bedroom. He headed toward the window like he was a gazelle with me locked, stunned, in his arms. With movements so quick I could barely see them, the vampire opened the window, thrust me through, and dangled me above the ground. My aching wrist was in his death grip (no pun intended). I flailed in midair while struggling not to scream.

"I've got you," he whispered quickly and climbed out the window after me. Closing it softly behind us, he gathered me in his arms again.

"Don't struggle, I don't want to hurt you," the vampire whispered as encased me tightly against his chest and leaped from the second floor window toward the manicured grass below. Once we hit the ground, we sprinted away so fast I felt as if my stomach was still up in the second floor bathroom.

* * *

"Sorry," he said with amusement while I threw up for the second time. We were about a half a mile from Ella and Bella Grayson's home underneath an enormous tree. I leaned against the trunk, grateful for the support.

"No problem," I choked out between retches.

"I think it's time that we visit Jeff Abernathy,"

the vampire told me. "When you're ready, of course."

"You mean rescue him?" I asked, panting. Jeeves handed me a bottle of water, and I accepted it gratefully. "Where did you get this?" I swished the water in my mouth and spit.

"No, I don't mean rescue him. And the water was on the desk in the bedroom. I grabbed it on the way out in case you had a reaction to my preferred method of travel."

"You couldn't get mouthwash?" I asked tartly. Straightening up, I turned toward the silent vampire. In the dimness of the evening and with distance, my attraction to Jeeves was no longer overwhelming. But it was there, nagging on the corners of my mind. "If we *visit* Jeff Abernathy, aren't we co-conspirators, technically?"

"We already *are*, technically. We know where Jeff is and haven't contacted the police. Well, no—I think it would be an accessory after the fact. Though, to be fair, we have not received, comforted, or assisted Zach and Brock in their kidnapping," Jeeves mused. "Generally speaking, there is legally no duty to rescue another person. We would have to knowingly *help* the person who has committed the felony to avoid arrest or trial. So no." He nodded to himself. "We have broken no law yet."

"You're just a walking criminal encyclopedia,

aren't you, Sparkles?" I asked him, shaking my head. "And sure we have. We just broke into a house."

Jeeves shrugged. "That's *barely* a crime. Trespassing at most. We took nothing other than that water bottle."

I stared.

The vampire stared back. "What?"

He talked about breaking the law and kidnapping in a tone so mild and matter-of-fact that it was a little disturbing. Martin and Jeeves had both insisted (at one time or another) that they were trying to break from Martin's mafia father. They both insisted Martin was trying to live a more legitimate life than his family legacy would suggest.

But who memorized the Arkansas criminal statutes other than attorneys and criminals?

"You're judging me again," Jeeves observed quietly. I didn't answer. "It's funny. I always have the feeling you're judging me, and, for some reason, I truly care that you are. Curious." He stepped forward, and bright white light from a streetlight bathed him. "I don't typically care what anyone other than Martin thinks."

"I'm not judging you," I lied.

"Really."

"Yep." I nodded.

"You are a fascinating creature, Fortuna. I often

feel like nothing I say will influence you, and yet I feel...compelled to keep trying."

"Oh, there are some things you can influence, all right," I said under my breath, and tossed the plastic bottle in a nearby recycling bin.

Jeeves stared unblinking—as if he hadn't heard. But I knew he did.

NINETEEN

A few texts back and forth with Pepper clarified that neither she nor Gabe would be any help. The two had gone to Claire's tiny apartment where Ollie was hiding out with Petey. Gabe wanted to let Ollie know that Miss Bessie was dead.

And...not.

Anyway, Spike had alerted Pepper through the *Ghosts, Ghosts Everywhere* app on her phone that he and Bella were still there, and that Bella seemed reluctant to leave the dog's side.

Why? I texted.

She feels like the dog is in danger, Pepper texted back. *And weirdly, it's not because of anything we've said to her. She's still a little out of it. Or the app translation just sucks.*

I wondered what that was about. *How's Gabe?*

Mad, she responded. *Like, really mad.* Pepper followed that statement with a red angry face emoji.

I couldn't blame him.

I wasn't exactly happy about the situation, either.

For all of Miss Bessie's harping on what I should do, had to do, was obligated to do? In the end, *she* chickened out of facing Gabe and telling him his own history. And what's more, she left *me* holding the bag for her with Gabe. He wouldn't be able to let loose on her for the years-long lie, and I had no doubt I would make a great stand-in.

"Martin is having drinks with Detective Conroe," Jeeves's deep voice broke through my worry. I looked up and expected to find him texting on his phone, but he wasn't.

"So?" I asked. I could hear the weariness in my own voice, but at least I wasn't throwing up anymore. "That's normal, right? I would think, anyway."

A passing car's headlights reflected in his intense eyes. "Ella Grayson is about to join them."

I forced myself not to roll my eyes. "Why is the Detective that arrested Azalea and the woman that murdered Bella Grayson having drinks with your boss?"

Jeeves's eyebrow raised at my calling Martin *your boss* and not by his name. "Detective Conroe found Petey's microchip in the clearing behind the gate and wanted to talk to Ella and Martin about the difficulty in tracing the dog." I raised my eyebrow. "Conroe believes that someone cut the identification out of the dog, and possibly its ear as well, considering."

Ew. "You and I both saw that greyhound," I said, frowning. "There wasn't a mark on him, so why would he think that?"

"No, there wasn't," Jeeves agreed without answering my question.

Oh, God...I hoped against hope that Jeeves wasn't regressing back to that barely speaking thing. That drove me crazy. "So someone planted Petey's microchip in the back clearing?" I tried again.

"Yes, likely without the chip ever being planted in the dog, since there was clearly no wound on the dog," he said and then paused. Jeeves dropped his face down and examined my shoes for a while—so long that I glanced down to make sure I hadn't upchucked on them. Moments later, the vampire cleared his throat—I didn't want to think about what he cleared it of. He waited until I was looking back at him to continue. "It was covered in blood, according to Martin. A lot of blood. Enough, Martin claims, to imply that the dog the blood came from was likely severely injured or dead."

I shuddered and tried to hold down the bile that rose up. I didn't even want to think about where Jeff Abernathy might have got *that* much greyhound blood, and I realized why Jeeves had been hesitant to tell me.

"Uh, this is all just horrible." I squatted down and put my head in my hands. "I hate this. Just hate this."

"Are you all right?" Jeeves asked, moving forward quickly.

"You know, for two people that claim to be trying to run the world's only *totally* almost-humane greyhound track? An *awful* lot seems to happen to the dogs living there," I snapped at him.

"Fortuna, look at me," Jeeves said quietly.

I kept my head in my hands.

"Fortuna, please. Please look at me."

This would almost be romantic if everything about it didn't turn my stomach. With a sigh and great trepidation about what I would hear next, I looked up.

"Greyhounds are universal blood donors. They have the dog equivalent of *golden* blood. Do you know what that is?" he asked me. I shook my head no. "Humans with golden blood have the rarest blood type in the world. It has no Rh antigens in it. Their blood is universal—they can donate to anyone, and so it's prized. Like those people, over eighty-five percent of greyhounds have a type of blood that can be used in *any* other dog safely."

"Thanks for the gore lesson, there, vampire," I said. "Your point?"

"One donation from a greyhound can save four other dogs," Jeeves continued patiently. "Taking blood from a greyhound is remarkably easy for the tech and the dog, so we encourage blood donation once a week at the track. Donations, incidentally, encourage the end of captive greyhound blood donors," he added, making sure I comprehended the philanthropic nature of this gesture. "In any case, the mobile blood unit comes once a week."

"So you're saying—"

"I'm saying that walking into the back of that bloodmobile and stealing a bag would not be a difficult thing to do. And the mobile blood van for donations was here just this morning. And finally," Jeeves sat back on his heels, "I can identify the owner of the blood by scent. I just need to get close to the microchip they found if we want to know for sure."

I blinked. "Wait, are you saying you know whose blood was on that syringe?"

Jeeves's eyes clouded, and his head tilted. "I can

tell you that the blood didn't belong to anyone alive within a five-mile radius of me at the time. Or now." Mystic's End was big, but not that big. That covered many people, almost the whole town—except anyone that might be at the track. "That indicates to me it was probably Bella's."

"You can track blood to its owner for five miles?"

He pointed to himself. "Vampire, remember? And that's not exact, but around there, yes." Jeeves reached out his hand and helped me back to my feet. Nausea itself had passed, but I was still feeling incredibly uncomfortable about all I learned concerning greyhound racing in general.

And, to be honest, Jeeves and Martin in particular.

"What now?" he asked.

"I don't know," I told him with an arched brow. "I feel like I'm missing something. Let's head back to the track."

Jeeves moved forward to grab me, and I scrambled away from him so desperately terrified that the vampire actually burst out laughing. "Come on, Fortuna, we'll be there in moments." He moved toward me again, and I ran behind the large tree.

"Let me rephrase that," I told him, peeking out from behind the trunk. "Call and get one of the limos to come and pick us up, please and thank you. We'll have it take us back to the track."

"My way is faster," Jeeves said, his arms wide open.

"*Car*, vampire," I snapped. "Please, and thank you. And don't touch me."

* * *

As we drove toward the Complex, I wondered where Miss Bessie had run off to. She hadn't followed us out of the house or tried to contact me in any way. That I noticed, anyway. With a shrug, I turned my attention back to the vampire sitting across from me. "Let's go over this."

"As you wish," Jeeves agreed with a nod.

"Here's what I think we know. Ella killed Bella. She got fentanyl from Jeff Abernathy and injected her. Petey's transfer was faked. Once he ran away, Ella and Jeff could both collect insurance policies on the dog. That was probably why they worked together," I said. "Maybe." I pulled my eyes from the ceiling toward Jeeves. "Would Jeff Abernathy really risk being a co-conspirator in a murder for only $45,000?"

"$75,000," Jeeves reminded me. "Jeff's policy was $75,000."

"Right, and then Bella had one," I remembered.

"And so did...wait a minute. You said all the transfer papers were fake."

"They were," Jeeves nodded. "Why?"

"Then who gets the insurance money from the policy for the buyer? You said the buyer was fake."

"No, I said the buyer was Jeff Abernathy," he corrected me. "The *company* was fake. Or, well, it was a real company able to accept money for Jeff Abernathy, but that was the only purpose."

"So, $120,000, then," I said, and nodded. "Yeah, I guess someone would kill for that."

"People *have* killed for less," Jeeves told me.

I just realized something. "Doesn't that mean Ella will get *less* money than Jeff Abernathy?"

"If Jeff never gave her the $45,000 as the fake Florida buyer, then yes, she would get less out of this monetarily than Abernathy," Jeeves nodded. "About half of what *he* would make from this entire endeavor. Though to be fair, she originally thought she was going to run off with all of Bella's assets."

"Right," I said nodding. I sat and thought about it, and all of it seemed tied up in a bow. The whole thing with Petey, though, still bothered me. "What I don't get is what they were going to *do* with Petey."

Jeeves looked at me with a cautious stare. "Well, I think it's pretty obvious, don't you?"

"Is it?" I asked him, crossing my arms. I understood what Jeeves was implying. Why bother doing anything with the dog? Just put it down, and collect the money. Easy. "Someone was *waiting* outside of the fence. Okay, sure, maybe they were going to catch Petey and put him down. But Petey's a greyhound. He's a *racing* greyhound. He's fast. Why risk him running away?"

"Maybe they just wanted witnesses to his disappearance to make the insurance claims easier."

"And Azalea getting arrested?" I asked him.

"I think that was just a coincidence."

"It was just a *coincidence* that they knew she was working with PeeGrrr the very morning Petey disappeared?"

"Fortuna, I think you overestimate the secrecy of the protest group," Jeeves smiled at me. "We all know who the members of the group are. They petition us on a variety of issues all the time. They're not some secret terrorist group. Their greatest strength is that they are incredibly, persistently annoying."

"It doesn't make any sense, though!" I crossed my arms. "I was there this morning. The dogs just *ran* off. Losing control of Petey amid this big conspiracy that seems to hinge on the dog just doesn't make any sense."

* * *

"Fortuna?" I turned and saw Hoyt Abernathy running up to us as soon as we exited the limo. "Have you found Pop?"

"No, Hoyt, sorry," I lied.

"Oh." His huge shoulders dropped. "I thought when I saw you coming back, that maybe you and Jeeves had..." His voice trailed off. "Anyway, I haven't heard from him. I haven't called the police, either, Mr. Jeeves," Hoyt assured Martin's bodyguard. "You tell Mr. Salvi I'm following his advice."

"I will, Mr. Abernathy," Jeeves assured him.

Ugh. For non-mafia people, this sure felt mafia-like.

"I found something, though, that might help," Hoyt handed two sheets of paper to Jeeves. Jeeves took the documents and scanned them both, frowning. "I thought it was weird, you know, because...well, I didn't find any tubes with their names on it and"—Hoyt glanced at me nervously —"I didn't think Fortuna liked us very much, so that seemed really confusing to me."

"What seemed confusing?" I asked.

No one answered me, but Hoyt continued babbling nervously at Jeeves. "I did check the sire freezer, you know, and there *is* a bucket for both of them and all. But no straws. If *Bella Bailout* was going to be transferred today, Mr. Jeeves, we would have needed to have straws already. I mean, if Pop was going to do that, right? So maybe that's what happened to him? Maybe someone came in and stole them?" he asked hopefully.

I stared back and forth between the two. It was like they were speaking another language. "What are you two talking about?"

"Hoyt, can you take me to the freezer?" Jeeves asked. Hoyt nodded and turned to go inside the Abernathy greyhound kennel.

"Could you tell me what's going on?" I asked Jeeves as I followed the two men.

"Just give me a moment, Fortuna," he answered without turning. "You may have been right that there was an aspect to all this we were missing."

"Great. What aspect?"

"Just hold on."

We followed Hoyt toward the back of the kennel and came to stand before a large upright freezer. It was old and beat up but huge, and the door contained a chain—as if what was stored inside was valuable.

The lock hanging from the chain was open.

With a tug, Hoyt opened the freezer, and fog poured out from it as the icy cold air hit the humid warmth. It looked like it was filled with white plastic buckets containing test tubes of some kind.

Each container had a name, and a date, and an amount of money written on it with a marker.

"See? Empty?" Hoyt told Jeeves, pointing to two buckets.

One bucket was marked *Bella Bailout*, and it had today's date.

The bucket next to it was marked *Gideon Jerubbesheth*. It also had today's date, but with another, smaller date underneath it.

Huh. That's bizarre. I wondered if Gideon had a brother with a similar name to him. The greyhound people did that sometimes, gave siblings similar names that differed by only one word.

Both buckets were marked $1500.

"I don't understand," I said, frowning. "What is this?"

"It's a freezer," Hoyt told me at a snail's pace as if I was a little slow on the uptake.

"I understand *that*, Hoyt," I said, not bothering to hide my annoyance. "But what do you *keep* in the freezer?"

"You know." He shifted uncomfortably. "Puppy stuff."

"Puppy stuff?" I was honestly perplexed.

He nodded. "Puppy stuff."

"Straws of greyhound sperm, Fortuna," Jeeves clarified. He went on somewhat haltingly. "People all over the country—and other countries as well—

will pay good money to have their dams—mother greyhounds—impregnated by a champion."

I stared at the freezer as my jaw dropped. "Holy crap, you people don't even let these poor dogs have sex?"

Three dogs from the kennel behind me barked sharply as if in agreement.

"The racing aspect is just one part of how these dogs make money," Jeeves explained. "If they do well, they can command large stud fees. An in-demand dog *can* be bred 20 to 50 times a month."

"A month?" Jeeves nodded. "One straw is one... um, attempt?" Jeeves nodded again, and I calculated quickly in my head. "Are you telling me this stuff can be worth $30,000 to $75,000 *a month?*" I gasped, my jaw dropping ever further. The vampire nodded a final time.

The insurance money wasn't the goal of this little plan. Well, the only goal.

This was the goal.

Jeff Abernathy wasn't going to *kill* Petey.

He was going to *breed* him.

Jeeves looked down at the papers in his hand, and I just knew there was even more.

"What are those papers?"

"Sire registrations, filled out this morning," Jeeves told me quietly. "One for Petey, and one..." Jeeves hesitated as if he knew the next thing he said would send me through the roof. Finally, he handed me a sheet of paper. "And one for your Gideon."

"What the bloody hell do you mean, one for Gideon?" I asked, snatching the paper from his hand. "No one ever asked me anything about this." I leaned in to reread Gideon's bucket. Today's date was prominent and easily readable.

Underneath was smaller and more challenging to read, but I knew it plain as I knew the nose on my face.

It was the date I bought Gideon.

Jeeves stared as if waiting for me to understand.

"They were going to kidnap the dogs and...Oh, dear lord, this place is an absolute horror show," I choked, shoving the piece of paper back at Jeeves. "Why *my* dog?"

"Daddy doesn't like you," Hoyt said, shrugging. I whirled on him and advanced menacingly, and his eyes widened. "Oh, no, I didn't know about this! I'm just sayin'! If what you and Mr. Jeeves say is real and you didn't agree to it, and Pop was gonna do it and stuff, I mean," Hoyt said, his words becoming confused. "Anyway, Pop hates you. And your dog."

"Was this just Jeff Abernathy, or was it Ella, too?" I asked Jeeves through clenched teeth.

"Her name's not on any of these papers," he responded after scanning them. "If I had to guess, she killed Bella, but Hoyt's father decided to take healthy advantage of the situation after assisting her. If they are partners in this, he hid the paper trail well."

"He hates that Ella woman, too," Hoyt offered.

"I'm going to kill him," I whispered fiercely.

"We have more than enough to have Mr. Abernathy arrested *and* convicted, Fortuna. But before we do that, we need to arrange a few things." Jeeves placed a gentle hand on my arm. "As for Ella Grayson, I have an idea on that, too."

"What?" I asked him angrily, still furious that someone would try and kidnap my dog, and then molest him. If it didn't involve turning her into a toad, I would handle it on my own.

As soon as I figured out how to turn someone into a toad.

Taking me in his arms so Hoyt couldn't hear, he pretended to console me. His voice whispered softly in my ear. "How do you feel about faking a psychic vision of a syringe in a bathroom?"

TWENTY

Of *course*, they were having drinks in *The Club*, Evangeline Leroux's spinning house of fine dining.

Because what I needed to add to this mix—besides the smokin' hot sandalwood scented vampire, the crotchety yet immature new ghost, the celibate runaway dog, and the newly unemployed resentful detective—was the vindictive, wine-soaked daughter of the Chief of Police who despised me.

Great.

"Fortuna," Martin purred in his smooth-as-butter voice. "So glad to see you and Jeeves decided to stop by. Detective Conroe, you remember Fortuna Delphi, don't you?"

Before Detective Conroe could answer, I heard a familiar voice behind me.

"What is *she* doing here? I would have expected her to be draped all over Gabe since he just lost that shrew of a grandmother." I turned to find a server weaving between Evangeline Laroux and me. The waitress's tray was held high, and her face tense as she tried to avoid colliding with her boss. Evangeline's perfectly manicured hand was wrapped around an abnormally large martini glass.

"Well, Angie, they just arrived here, so we don't quite know yet," Martin told her. Turning to Jeeves and me, Martin asked if we'd like to sit down.

"Don't mind if I do," Angie Laroux answered and made a beeline for Martin. Infused with the brazen confidence born of plastic surgery and expensive booze, Evangeline draped herself across Martin's lap. She placed her arm around him to ensure that her costly bosoms pressed against him. "The most comfortable place in the house, I'd say," she cooed.

Martin's expression didn't change at all as he adjusted his arm around her. Detective Conroe was practically panting as the Mystic's End Marilyn Monroe nearly spilled out of her sheer gown.

"Jeeves, Fortuna, sit down," Martin invited again.

Jeeves (rather rudely) sat down first without

pulling out my chair, but when he gestured toward his lap with a wry eyebrow raise, it was all I could do not to slap him. "No, thanks. I'm good in a chair." I yanked out the seat next to him with a glare. He chuckled.

The linen tablecloth was covered in a collection of shot glasses and half-empty cocktails.

My guess was Evangeline had been at this table previously.

"So, as I was saying, Martin," the detective tore his eyes reluctantly from Angie's ample breasts, "we're just not sure where to look for the dog. I hope it doesn't cause you too many problems here at the track."

"Detective Conroe, you're aware that Fortuna was a fortune teller before she arrived in Mystic's End." Jeeves leaned forward and ignored Evangeline Leroux's fingers gently outlining Martin's chest muscles.

"Yes, I had heard that," Conroe answered.

"Your skin is so *soft*, Martin," Angie breathed leaning into him. I glanced over and saw that her hand was inside his button-down shirt. "And you smell just like that Indian incense my college roommate used to get." Leaning forward, she nuzzled into his neck, closed her eyes, and breathed deeply. "It's positively *divine*."

"I didn't think you attended college, Angie," I observed.

Evangeline Laroux shot me a dirty look. Martin glanced at me as if concerned—or hopeful—that I would be jealous.

Fat chance.

"Well, I thought that—if you were at an impasse —it might not hurt to have Fortuna give you a reading on the situation," Jeeves told Conroe. "Perhaps she has the gift after all and can give you a clue to follow."

The two men debated the reliability of psychic visions. At the same time, Evangeline Laroux continued to paw at Martin like he was a piece of meat.

* * *

"Gentleman, I *told* you I have a plane to catch," the haughty Ella Grayson said as she stepped up to the table. "What is this about?"

"Mrs, Grayson," Detective Conroe nodded. "If we find your animal—"

"If you find the dog, fine. If you don't, insurance will take care of any money that I'm out. Now, *what* was so important that I needed to come here in person?"

"Before you leave town, we'll just need you to

sign the guardianship of the dog over to the track so
I can continue to manage the situation," Martin
said. He twisted beneath Evangeline Laroux and
pulled out an envelope from his interior jacket
pocket. "You can also appoint someone else to
handle the situation here if you like, but since you'll
be out of contact, it's important someone is
empowered to handle what's happening. You know,
should anything change."

Ella snatched the extended envelope, pulled the
contents out, and briefly scanned it. "What do you
think would *change*, Mr. Salvi?" Ella asked.

"Well, the dog could turn up for one," I told
her. "And he could turn up before the Graysons'
attorney gets a court order giving the dog to Claire,
his rightful owner now." Ella Grayson froze, and
the color drained from her face. "You wouldn't
want poor Petey to end up in a shelter, would
you?"

"I don't care *where* that mutt ends up," she
snapped. She pulled out a fancy gold pen and
signed the guardianship papers using Detective
Conroy's back as a table. With an aggravated
flourish, she tossed them down on the dining table
among the empty glasses. "Are we done? Is that
all?"

"I'm gonna miss you, Ella-wella," Angie Laroux
slurred. She pushed against Martin, struggling to

get up, and then collapsed back down on him with a girlish giggle. Instead, she waved.

"My God, Angie, you're a *complete* mess," Ella snapped.

"It's late!" Evangeline responded brightly. "I'm always drunk when it's late!"

I stood up and extended my hand. "I just want to apologize again for letting the dog run off, Mrs. Grayson," I told her. She looked down at my hand with a pinched face and paused. Then she reluctantly extended her hand.

We clasped.

Showtime.

I took a deep breath, threw my head back, rolled my eyes back, and tried to vibrate as if I was being struck by a compelling vision. "Behold, I see it!" I shouted. I could feel Ella struggle to pull her hand out of mine, but I gripped her more tightly. The murmuring of hundreds of customers got quieter, and quieter still, and then stopped altogether as I continued to fake my vision.

"Let go of me!" Ella shouted.

"I see a wife betrayed. Greed, oh, *such* greed!" I wailed, shaking my head back and forth. "A healthy, beautiful woman felled by...by something silver! Silver and glass! Yes, yes, I see it! A needle plunged into a healthy body, a needle that brings death for greed! Oh, it's terrible! Horrible!" I cried, gasping.

"The needle, the evidence of murder most foul! It's in the master bathroom of your home! You!" I shouted, yanking my hand from hers. "*You* killed Bella Grayson! It was you!"

With a final cry, I collapsed on the chair as if I passed out.

As I lay there, my eyes closed, I could hear footsteps racing from the table, the detective on the phone calling for officers to get over to Ella and Bella's home immediately.

I fluttered my eyes open to find Jeeves standing over me as if concerned for my health. He was staring at me, a wry grin on his face.

"That was quite a performance," he whispered.

"Anything worth doing is worth doing well," I whispered back.

* * *

The entire dining room was staring at me, patrons speaking in low voices as if they didn't want to be overheard. The waitstaff flew from one end of the restaurant to another carrying tray upon tray of the most potent drinks *The Club* offered.

"I don't know what I just saw, Miss Delphi," Detective Conroe said, "but we still have an active search warrant for Bella Grayson's home. If your, ah, vision was real and Bella was really murdered, we'll find that murder weapon."

"Hope so, Detective," I nodded. "What about Ella Grayson? Are you going to stop her from leaving town?"

Beau Conroe looked at the three of us—sans Evangeline Laroux, who was now at the bar pouring shot after shot down her gullet—with a wary look on his face. "I can't do anything until we find and test that syringe, Miss Delphi. As far as I know, Mrs. Grayson died of natural causes."

"But she didn't," I blurted out without thinking. "Talk to Ollie Kane. He—"

"Fortuna, did you see Ollie Kane in your vision?" Jeeves's cut me off before I offered information I wasn't supposed to have. Heck, Ollie wasn't even supposed to have it, but considering his boss's laissez-faire attitude toward his job—and that Ollie had brought the information to him first—he'd probably make it through okay.

Especially considering who his father was.

"Yes, yes," I nodded. "You should talk to Ollie Kane about Bella Grayson. I think you'll find that he thought there might be more to the story than simple early death."

"Will do." Detective Conroe tipped his hat and left.

"Ella Grayson is still on the property," Jeeves

told Martin. "She's making her way to the third parking deck. Do you want me to do anything about that?"

"Go make sure that she doesn't know anything that would hurt the track," Martin told him, his voice low.

Jeeves nodded. *Hopefully, it won't come to that,* the vampire responded to Martin telepathically after a brief pause.

I didn't know what that meant, or how Jeeves would make sure of that. I assumed the vampire could just walk by her and read her mind, but there was something...*ominous* about exchange. A hint of danger that Martin was doing his best to hide from me. My stomach dropped.

"I'm coming," I insisted. I couldn't stand the woman, but I didn't want anyone else getting hurt.

"No," Martin said firmly. "That's *not* happening."

"No bottles," I shot back. I stepped up to him, my eyes narrowing. "If Jeeves needs to talk to Ella, he does it *with* me there, or that bottle doesn't get opened. And not *just* that one. None of them. Not as long as I'm the mystic. Your choice. You want something from me? Well, I want something from you."

Martin stared at me, his brows knitting together in frustration, his handsome face lined with disapproval at my demand. He even looked a little angry. It was clear Martin Salvi was not used to anyone challenging him—I'd seen his master-of-the-universe act more than once since I met him. "This isn't a game, Fortuna."

"This was never a game, Martin," I answered. Then I yawned and looked at my phone. Only nine-thirty at night? Jeez. This was literally the longest day of my entire life. It felt like it'd lasted three days.

Martin handed Jeeves the stack of papers Ella had signed. "Fine. Take her," he said while casting another disapproving glance at me.

As if I needed his approval.

"Yes, sir." Jeeves grabbed my hand and pulled me out of the club. Once we were far enough away from Martin that he couldn't overhear, the vampire murmured, "You're not going to like how we get there, though."

* * *

I didn't throw up this time. So, progress.
      Jeeves and I beat Ella to her car—the car Jeeves found by scent alone.

Which was creepy.

"She's coming," he murmured.

And within a minute, she did.

"Get away from my car!" Ella shouted and clicked the remote to unlock it. She was storming toward us as if in a rage.

"No," I said. "You're going to prison—"

"I'm going on a plane—"

"You're not, though," I said, tugging a hand through my flat hair that was desperately in need of a hairbrush. "I want to know if you knew that Jeff Abernathy was going to kidnap my dog, too, as part of your little plan."

"What are you talking about?" she snapped, genuinely confused.

Jeeves and I glanced at each other. "Did she really not know?" he asked me.

"How would I—"

Jeeves raised an eyebrow.

"Oh, right," I smiled and turned back to Ella.

Walking toward her, I opened myself up to her thoughts, emotions, and memories. I sifted through a torrent of greedy horror. The anger she had at Bella for continuing the friendship with Claire. The resentment she had for having to fake affection for Bella just to have access to her money. How much she despised Petey because Bella was obsessed with the greyhound. And the glee she felt when Evangeline Laroux introduced her to Jeff Abernathy—who promised he could help her take care of her problem.

I gasped. "Did Evangeline Laroux know that you were going to kill your wife?"

"Yeah, well, she *wasn't* my wife, now, was she?" Ella answered ferociously, her anger loosening any brakes she might have had on her mouth. "That stupid woman made sure that I would be screwed if I ever tried to leave her."

"Or kill her, clearly," I pointed out.

"Well, I didn't know that, *did* I?" she snapped. "And anyway, Angie didn't know anything about anything. Honestly, that woman's barely sober enough to remember her own damn name."

I analyzed Ella as she talked. Her hatred of the greyhound, wanting him dead, going to Jeff Abernathy, and offering to pay him if he would just cause the dog to have a deadly accident, her vengeance on Bella. His handing her the fentanyl bottle and the syringe so she could kill her wife. His urging that it would be fine, that she needed to so they could both share in the bounty that would come from her widowhood.

"He convinced you to kill Bella," I whispered.

"Shut up," she snapped at me. "You people and your obsession with these stupid dogs," she raged in a fury. "You care about them like they're something more than galloping money bags. They're not. It's disgusting. You and your little assistant and your stupid love of these filthy creatures. They're nothing but dumb animals, too stupid to care or suffer—"

"Shut up," I whispered, advancing on her. "You're a killer. Every dog at this track probably has a better moral compass than you—"

Ella shoved me, hard. "Get out of my way!"

I...think I snapped.

I was swimming in a pool of hate and greed and resentment, all coming from Ella Grayson. When she grabbed me to push me out of her way, it exploded in me like a volcano erupting. I grabbed her by the throat and shoved her against the car, my eyes narrow, my teeth clenched.

"Get...off...me..." she rasped.

"I wish you knew what these dogs go through. Caged almost all day," I told her, looking back and forth, deep into her eyes. "The risk of death if they don't run fast enough, robbed of everything it means to be a dog. No freedom. No family. No relationships. But that *wasn't* enough for you," I told her menacingly as we slid lower toward the parking deck. "No, you had to try and destroy Petey's life because you're a vicious, vindictive—"

"Um, Fortuna," Jeeves said politely, but I ignored him.

"If I had my way, I'd forgo prison and condemn you to life as the dog you tried to kill," I told her. "Prison is too good for you. Prison would let you out of your cage more than these dogs get let out."

I was so angry I didn't hear the buzzing in my ear. Or see the glow that surrounded us. Or notice that Ella Grayson was getting shorter. And shorter.

And shorter.

By the time I realized what was happening, a flash of light blinded me. When my vision cleared and the fury had drained out of me, Petey was standing in front of me. The dog was in a panic, yowling and snapping and jumping.

I stood back up and stared. Then I looked at Jeeves. "What the hell just happened?"

Jeeves looked at me with amusement. "I believe you turned her into a dog, oh great mystic." He tilted his head and examined Petey-Ella. "A frog would have been more portable, but this works, too."

TWENTY-ONE

I tried multiple times to return Ella back to human form. There was a problem with that. Since I wasn't sure how I'd turned her into a carbon copy of Petey, I wasn't entirely sure how the heck to change her back. The dog continued to panic, snap, and snarl.

"We don't have time to keep trying. We'll leave the dog with Hoyt," Jeeves said finally, "and then go visit Jeff Abernathy and his captors. If all goes well, we can bring this whole affair to a close by midnight."

I looked at my phone. Just two hours, and this hideous day would come to a close. "How's that? And won't Hoyt just call the police?"

"Not if I tell him not to," Jeeves deadpanned.

He grabbed Petey-Ella's collar and gave him/her a sharp *shhhh*. Pulling out his phone, he called someone for a golf cart with a dog crate and then hung up. "I think you underestimate the loyalty that people have toward Martin, Fortuna."

"I don't underestimate it," I disagreed and leaned against a concrete pillar. "I just don't understand it."

"It's true that Martin is trying to step away from his father's legacy. But there are some things his father taught him that will stick with him. Loyalty and protection for those that show loyalty to him is one of those things." Jeeves looked at me with a mixture of doubt and vigilance. "It was something I hoped you would come to count on. Though today, it seems like you are more forcefully rejecting it than you ever have before," he observed (not incorrectly). "Why?"

"I don't trust him. I told you that."

"It's more than that."

"I don't like what he does," I added. "I told you that, too."

Jeeves raised his eyebrow. "It must be more than that."

"Why? Why would I need more than that?"

"You went out with him," Jeeves pointed out. "Those two minor things couldn't possibly have derailed your friendship and romantic relationship."

"Those are *not* minor things. You don't know many women, do you?" I asked him. I pushed myself off the pillar and stood taller, meeting Jeeves's gaze directly. "Look, people's motivations are important, and Martin's motivations for everything he's done for me or with me—they're as opaque as ever. Sure, I know him better—and yet the more I know him, the less I know him. Each thing I learn leads to three more questions, and each thing he reveals argues against something he said to me in the past. Everything he does with me just breeds mistrust."

Jeeves stared at me, his expression blank as a new canvas. We looked at one another, and I felt a tiny flash, just a flash, of extreme frustration. Was I pushing through his defenses, or was he so frustrated that his feelings were leaking through them?

I didn't have time to think about it. The golf cart pulled up, and we were off to put Petey-Ella in the greyhound kennel.

* * *

"Do you think you'll be able to change the dog back?" Jeeves asked as we pulled up in front of my shop. Gideon's face was pressed against the front window. The numerous dog nose smears told me that Gideon wasn't thrilled about being left back in the shop alone without even a ghost for company.

Unfortunately, Jeeves and I weren't headed for the shop.

We were headed for the old courthouse.

"What's the plan?" I asked as we walked across the street.

"I'll talk to Brock and Zach if they're there, Jeff Abernathy if they aren't." I waited, but ten steps later, Jeeves hadn't bothered to elaborate.

"About?"

Ten more steps. No response. I looked around, but I didn't see the white van.

"See, this is why my level of trust is super-low," I murmured.

"Can you do me a favor?" Jeeves asked as we reached the door. "Can you refrain from turning anyone into an animal while we're in there?"

"Ha ha, very funny."

"I wasn't trying to be funny," the vampire told me, opening the door for me.

His steps were silent, but he didn't creep or motion at me to be quiet. We walked down the stairs, through the hallways, and Jeeves turned the corner, marching into the old jailhouse cell area like he owned the place.

"Finally!" Jeff Abernathy called out raspingly when he spotted the vampire. He struggled to his feet, jerking when the chains didn't give him enough room to stand upright. "Quick, get me out of these things before they come back!"

"That's not why we're here," Jeeves told the disheveled man. He grabbed an old metal chair, pulled it a few feet in front of Abernathy, and sat down. "We're here because Martin is extremely disappointed in you, Mr. Abernathy. You've caused problems for the track. As you well know, that's not something that's tolerated."

"I didn't cause no problems for nobody!" he shouted hotly, but the kennel owner's face was drained of color. "I've been kidnapped, you idiot! How did *I* cause this?"

"Yes, you were kidnapped by Brock Grayson and Zach Johnson," Jeeves nodded. "Because you assisted Ella Grayson in her quest to murder her wife, Bella. And then you planned to hide her dog *and* kidnap Fortuna's dog so that you could profit off stud fees for years—without having to give either owner their cut."

"I...I wasn't gonna...You can't think..." Abernathy's stuttered and tripped over his denials as if he wasn't sure which accusation to argue against first.

"You were, I can, and now we have some issues to work out, Mr. Abernathy," Jeeves told him, nodding. He pulled out papers and held them up. "You're going to sign your kennel over to your son, Hoyt, and you're going to confess your crimes to your friend, Chief Clutterbuck. You will plead guilty to whatever they choose to charge you with to ensure there is no investigation and no trial."

"The hell I will!" he shouted.

"I apologize, Mr. Abernathy, perhaps I should have made it clear at the beginning," Jeeves said, standing up. "I wasn't offering you a choice in the matter."

"What the hell are you even here for?" Jeff Abernathy turned toward me.

"Fortuna was instrumental in uncovering what you had done," Jeeves answered for me.

"It was all Ella!" he protested, looking frantic. "I didn't do anything. It was all her fault!"

"Ella Grayson is gone," Jeeves told him—somewhat truthfully—without missing a beat. "There is no one else to blame here, Mr. Abernathy. You are the last man standing, and you will take the fall to protect what you, and others, have built. You will confess the truth so everything is explained away."

"Oh yeah? And if I don't?" Abernathy snarled.

Jeeves held his hand to his chest and bowed slightly. "I apologize again, Mr. Abernathy. I keep believing myself to be clear, but I keep forgetting you've had a bit of a stressful day. Again, you have no choice in the matter. I'm telling you how this situation will come to a close."

"I won't do it," Jeff said, mustering up every bit of courage he had to defy the vampire.

With a sigh, Jeeves nodded. "Very well."

And then he jumped toward Jeff Abernathy so quickly, the man barely had time to react.

* * *

We were sitting in the police precinct twenty minutes later. A few radios crackled, an officer walked by now and again, but for the most part, the building was quiet.

"And that's the whole story," Jeff Abernathy told Detective Conroe and Chief Clutterbuck. Jeff Abernathy smiled proudly as if awaiting a medal.

The two exhausted, rumpled men stared at Jeff Abernathy, stunned.

"Oh, I returned the dog back to the kennel," he nodded eagerly. "I realized the error of my ways and everything. And now, I want to confess and plead guilty and serve my time and stuff. Right now. I don't need a lawyer. Can we get a judge here?" he asked.

"You," Chief Clutterbuck drawled suspiciously, toying with a huge cup of coffee. "*You* realized the error of your ways."

"I did, I did," Abernathy nodded, gung-ho to start his prison term. "You should drop the charges against Azalea Cotton. She didn't do anything. I opened the gate. That was me," he smiled excitedly. "I was hoping that I could knock out two birds with one fentanyl bottle and get PeeGrrr out of my hair as well as make all sorts of money from the dog stud fees. Not to mention the insurance money when you declared the dog dead. Ooh, that's a fraud, too! You have to charge me with fraud!"

"Are you on drugs?" Detective Conroe asked him.

"Nope, confession is good for the soul, right?" Abernathy responded with a huge smile.

"Book him," Clutterbuck told Conroe, standing up and crushing the styrofoam coffee cup in his right hand. "How did you come across him?" the chief asked Jeeves and me.

"Just lucky, I suppose, Chief," Jeeves responded. The chief waited for a further explanation, but the vampire said nothing more.

Clutterbuck eyed us both distrustfully. "I'm not

hiring your boy toy back if that's what you're hoping."

"I don't have a boy toy, sir, but if you're talking about Gabe, that's really between you and him."

"Wow. You finally found something in this town you don't think concerns you, Miss Delphi?" Clutterbuck chuckled with a raised eyebrow. "I'm impressed."

I fought the urge to turn him into a frog.

"Well, Mr...Mr..." Clutterbuck seemed confused when he couldn't remember Jeeves's last name.

"Jeeves, sir," the vampire responded.

"Right," he rolled his eyes. "I don't know that I believe a word any of y'all have told me, but it fits, and it doesn't cause me any problems, so we'll go with it," he said, grabbing his keys off the desk. "I'm going home to get some sleep. I'll have someone go by Azalea Cotton's in the morning to let her know she's not a suspect anymore. We can get that ankle bracelet back, too."

"What about Ella Grayson?" I asked.

"We have a warrant out for her arrest now," Detective Conroe told me. "We found the needle, and the coroner handed over the tests his assistant had done. She was supposed to be on a plane out of Little Rock tonight, but airport police let us know she never got on it. I suspect she knew the jig was up and hightailed it out of town some other way."

Or...she didn't.

"We'll catch her eventually," Chief Clutterbuck said. Then he eyed me suspiciously. "Real convenient, you having your 'psychic vision' and all, Miss Delphi, right where Detective Conroe and a whole gaggle of tourists could see it."

"Oh, they're never convenient, sir," I told him. "It was actually kind of embarrassing."

"Was it now?" The Chief's face looked highly skeptical. "You don't look very embarrassed."

"I'm just glad the right people were caught— since your department seemed to have the whole thing completely wrong from the very beginning," I responded innocently.

His jawed dropped, and then he laughed.

"And on that, I'm going home," Clutterbuck said as he turned on his heel.

* * *

"We made a good team," Jeeves said as we left the police precinct. The moon was high in the sky, and the stars in the clear night sparkled.

"We did," I nodded. "Even though you only helped to get me to go with you to look in that hole behind the track. And you stayed involved to protect Martin and the track, not out of any desire to see justice done. So, it wasn't exactly selfless on your part, was it?"

The vampire stopped and turned to look at me. He didn't respond.

"What are we going to do about Brock and Zach?" I asked him.

"I'll take care of them."

"By hypnotizing them," I guessed.

"Can you think of a better way to tie up the loose threads dangling from this fiasco of a day?" he asked me gently. "I *could* kill them, but I feel like you'd be averse to that course of action."

I gasped. "Why would you kill them?"

"I wouldn't, really," he shrugged, giving me a wry smile. "I just wanted to see your reaction. I'll remove the memory of their crime from their minds. You mentioned that they were never violent with him, and they wouldn't have killed him."

"No, I didn't think they would," I agreed. I yawned again. "Man, I am so tired. I can't believe all this happened over one single day. Sleepy small town, my rear end."

"You should go home and get some sleep," Jeeves said, stepping closer. "You look exhausted. I can go over to Claire's home and explain to those there what's transpired." He looked down. "They all know you're a witch?"

"Yes. Claire just found out today, but yes," I nodded and yawned again. "Why?"

"I needed to know whether I could explain to them what happened to Ella."

"What about the trip down a deep, dark hole that I owe you?" I asked him.

Jeeves's head snapped forward, and I could see in his eyes that he heard my statement as a distinctly different one than I had intended. Blood flushed his cheeks pink.

Jeez. Men.

"The hole with the *ladder*, vampire," I told him forcefully.

"We'll talk tomorrow," Jeeves assured me. "You need some sleep."

He was right. I was swaying on my feet.

Gathering me in his arms, he took me home, depositing me directly in bed so quickly, the frantic, crazy day seemed a little bit like a dream. I heard Gideon race up the stairs and jump on the bed.

I was asleep before he slithered in next to me.

TWENTY-TWO

"Oh, no," I told Gideon, who trotted after me with wide, hopeful eyes. "I warned you that you weren't getting any bacon from me after what you did yesterday. Some loyal hound *you* are." Gideon snorted happily and hopped forward to press his head affectionately against my thigh. "Sucking up isn't going to change anything, Gid. I'm still very unhappy with you."

I placed the plate of bacon and eggs down on the counter and turned to refill my coffee. I'd barely wrapped my hand around the pot before I heard the plate crash to the ground—followed by the sound of clawed paws scampering away. "You know, Gideon," I said with exhaustion, "I can turn things into *other* things now. How do you feel about being a frog?"

"Have you figured out how to control that transmutation power you discovered?" a deep voice from the stairway called. I turned to find Martin climbing up the stairs to the second floor—shadowed by his pet vampire. As if they owned the place.

"Did you sleep well, Fortuna?" Jeeves asked politely.

"You know, the two of you don't have walk-in privileges to my home," I told them coldly.

"I used to," Martin responded.

"Yep, you used to," I nodded. "Now, you don't."

Martin frowned. "I apologize if I overstepped."

I shrugged. "What do you want, Martin?"

I looked at the handsome man, a man I once thought I could care about, and wondered what on earth I had possibly seen in him. Why was it so easy to mistake manipulative and calculating behavior for sexy? Sure, he could be charming, but I was pretty sure he'd never been charming without an agenda.

He cleared his throat. "Now that the situation with the missing greyhound is over, I had hoped that you would accompany Jeeves to the shaft that only you and he can see," Martin said politely while tugging on his collar—as if it had become uncomfortably tight. "We thought the two of you could set out early so that you could open the shop on time."

"No," I deadpanned.

Martin appeared shocked. "Did you say no?"

"That's right, I said no," I repeated.

Martin seemed so dumbfounded by my outright refusal he was rendered speechless.

"May I ask why?" Jeeves asked quietly.

"I have two friends that just lost people they love," I told him. "Gabe lost his grandmother last night, and Claire lost someone she loved, to murder. Miss Bessie has just crossed over. I ran around town helping you all day yesterday, and I'm needed elsewhere—"

Martin held up a hand. "Not to correct you, Fortuna, but Jeeves was helping you—"

"No, Martin, Jeeves was clearly helping *you*," I snapped back impatiently. "Just like everything else in this town, everything tied back to the track and money in the end. Azalea might have been threatened, but *you* were, too. I don't know what abyss you're afraid to fall into, but you,"—I pointed at Jeeves—"seemed to be willing to kill last night to keep him,"—I pointed back at Martin — "from falling into it. And that wasn't about Azalea."

"It's just business," Martin responded.

"And anyone who gets involved with you has to accept that, right? Well, I won't."

Martin shot a frustrated glance at Jeeves. "I thought you said she agreed to help?"

"Hey, Martin?" I raised my voice. "I'm standing right here. Talk to *me*."

His eyes swiveled back toward me and narrowed.

"I agreed to help yesterday, but right now, I'm regretting that. So, here's what we're going to do. You're going to agree to end greyhound racing in Mystic's End. And you're going to do it without a single, solitary dog being harmed, abandoned, or euthanized."

Martin's eyes grew wide. "You *can't* be serious."

"I'm totally serious. You and I will map out the steps you need to take to shut racing down here. When I'm satisfied you've made progress, I'll help you with something. If you do something behind my back, a dog gets hurt, a kennel puts a dog down because they're too cheap to house it until it's adopted, my help with the witch bottles stops. Completely. For *good*."

"That's incredibly manipulative," Jeeves observed. I couldn't tell if he was impressed or disgusted.

"Well, I've been learning from the best." I shrugged. "Do we have a deal?"

"We *had* a deal yesterday," Martin said.

"Then I'm renegotiating terms," I responded.

Martin turned away from me and walked to my window. He looked down over the town of Mystic's End, a city he thought he had entirely in his control. His eyes danced this way and that—as if the mafia prince was mentally running through all the scenarios in which he could get what he wanted *without* giving me what I wanted. Finally, he gave a single decisive nod of his head, turned on his heel, and made for the stairs.

"That was unexpected," Jeeves told me quietly.

"If so, clearly, neither one of you know me very well."

Without small talk or even a goodbye, Jeeves, too, nodded and left.

* * *

I knocked on the door to Gabe's house and wasn't surprised when Pepper opened the door.

"Come on in," she gestured. "He's doing better, but he's still...he's not happy."

Ollie and Claire were sitting on the couch watching a morning talk show. Petey (the real one) lay at Claire's feet with his chin on her shoe. "Fortuna," she said softly when she spotted me. "Jeeves told us what happened. Thank you so much for what you did. I know it can't bring Bella back," she smiled sadly, and the dog whined in agreement. "But at least the people who hurt her will pay the price for it."

"Where is Bella?" I asked, looking around.

"Upstairs with Spike and Aunt Bessie. I think they're trying to calm Gabe down or communicate with him, or something, but...well, you'll see." At once, Claire's face filled with concern, sadness—and a little apprehension.

I looked at Pepper.

"So, Gabe wouldn't download the app because he didn't want to talk to Miss Bessie yet," Pepper said, ushering me toward the stairs. "The good news is, I think if she wants to be a poltergeist in the afterlife she clearly has the skills for it."

I swallowed and hurried faster up the steps.

Pushing the bedroom door open, I gasped.

Gabe's bedroom was a *disaster*.

Bulbs were broken, pictures, and cologne bottles in disarray. Two lay broken on the floor, and they filled the room with a chokingly heavy scent of woodsy musk. Drawers were half-open, and Gabe's underwear hung from the chandelier, the mirror, and the headboard.

"You need to talk to me, young man!" Miss Bessie hollered as Spike and Bella stared at her, wide-eyed. Gabe sat on the bed, head in his hands. I gasped again as I surveyed the destruction, and the detective raised his head and stared at me, his eyes pleading.

"Please make her stop," Gabe asked me wearily. "I don't think she can hear me."

Oh, she heard him, all right.

"Miss Bessie!" I told the ghost sharply. "This is no way to behave!"

"Don't you tell me what to do!" Miss Bessie screeched, flinging another pair of tighty-whities across the room. "You tell that boy to install that *Ghosts, Ghosts Everywhere* app so I can talk to him or so help me, there will be ghosts, ghosts everywhere for every minute remaining in his life!"

"Miss Bessie, stop and think about what this would look like to someone still alive," I told her, my hands on my hips. "He can't hear you. All he can see is the wanton destruction of every item in his bedroom!" A rubber-ducky patterned bathrobe flew across the room. "Miss Bessie!"

"Can we go?" Spike asked nervously.

Bella nodded frantically. "Yes, please. Please, Fortuna, can you take over?"

"You're such a nut you've scared the other ghosts, Miss Bessie. That's not a great way to make a first impression, is it?" I picked up the rubber-ducky robe.

"Don't talk to me like I'm an old lady!"

"I'm not. I'm talking to you like a child because that's what you're acting like." At once, Miss Bessie's glowing ghost face was filled with indignation. "Look at Gabe, Miss Bessie. Is this how you want him to feel? *Look* at him. Look at what you're doing to him."

The old woman looked at Gabe, her face now filled with concern. She floated over to him and wrapped her arms around him, but they simply passed through him. Her face fell. "I just want him to talk to me. I can explain everything if he would just *talk* to me."

"Let me talk to him. It's less effort, and it's easier. We'll get you and Gabe hooked up on the app when he's ready. Can you let me do that?" I asked her. I took care to keep my voice gentle to prevent the old woman from going off on Gabe's underwear drawer again.

"Can I trust you?" Miss Bessie asked me earnestly.

"Trust me, Miss Bessie," I told her. "Delphi Coven bond, right? Just let me talk to him."

"All right," the old woman answered finally. "The ghosts and I will be downstairs."

"No more throwing things," I warned her.

She tried to clutch my hand, but again, her limbs simply passed through. Pausing, the old woman's specter looked back at Gabe. Her incorporeal eyes were no longer capable of watering, but if they were, there would be tears in them. "Make sure he knows I was only trying to protect him. Make sure he knows I love him," she told me.

"I will," I promised again.

* * *

It took a bit to get Pepper out of the bedroom, but finally, Gabe and I were alone.

"Nice bedroom," I told him casually. Holding up his bathrobe, I smiled. "I didn't figure you for rubber duckies, but I like it. Very stylish." I laid the robe carefully over a chair in the corner, and then sat down to face him. "Are you okay?"

"For someone who's had their world torn apart? Sure," Gabe shrugged, flashing me a drained smile. "I feel like I should make a joke about finally getting you into my bedroom, but to tell you the truth, I just don't have the energy."

I smiled sympathetically. "It's been a hard twenty-four hours."

"It's been a cataclysmic twenty-four hours," he corrected. Raising his head, the former detective looked me in the eye. My heart broke a little. Gabe looked *so* tired, with deep lines on his face and bags under his eyes. "Yesterday morning, I had a career and a family. Today, I have none of those things."

"Clearly, your family hasn't gone anywhere," I joked, pointing to the destruction Miss Bessie had wrought in her afterlife temper tantrum. He chuckled weakly, but the glum sadness soon returned. "Look, Gabe, I can't pretend to know how you feel. I can't. But I can tell you that Miss Bessie loves you."

"Then how could she keep all this from me?" he whispered, his voice cracking.

"I think she thought she was doing it to protect you," I told him. "I don't know if she was right to do it, or she was wrong to do it. But I can tell you I'm completely sure she thought what she was doing was the best thing for you."

"And leaving me?" His voice was hurt, a small boy's wound.

I took a quick intake of breath and slumped. "I think maybe that's my fault."

He looked at me, surprised. "Your fault?"

"When she made me the mystic, I...I really didn't care," I admitted reluctantly. "I had just become a witch and didn't really know what that meant, and what she gave me didn't really seem to be a big deal to me at all. I wasn't...wasn't diligent in finding out its meaning. Talking to her about it.

Letting her train me. Hearing her stories. I pushed it aside," I told him. "A lot."

"You think that's why she...um, she died?" Gabe asked.

"I think it was a lot of things. I know she didn't like you being with the police department, and your getting fired solved a concern for her. I *do* think, since you have to start a new career and all, that she wanted to make whatever you do next financially easier on you. Inheritance helps, right? But mostly? I think she wants to help find your mom's witch bottle, and she knew she'd be able to do that better as a ghost."

"Maybe," Gabe admitted. His face had more color in it, and he didn't look quite so defeated. "How can she help you more as a ghost?"

"Does it look like she's capable of being ignored as an incorporeal being?" I asked, sweeping my arm toward the disaster in his bedroom. "When she was alive, I could just not return her calls if I didn't want to deal with her, or the town curse, or the coven history. Now that she's dead? I'm pretty screwed."

He laughed.

"Unless you want to be picking your underwear out of the light fixtures for weeks, you should install the ghost app on your phone," I told him. "Besides, woe unto you if you get the wrong flowers for your grandmother at her funeral."

Gabe sighed, nodded, and pulled out his phone.

* * *

"What happens now?" Pepper asked as we stepped back into the living room.

"Now, we let Miss Bessie and Gabe have some time to themselves," I told her, glancing at Gabe. "I think they have a lot to talk about, and it will take some time for Miss Bessie to get the hang of communicating without throwing anything."

"Is he still mad at me?" Miss Bessie asked, rather snottily.

"Go talk to him," I told her.

"You better not be setting me up, missy," Miss Bessie snapped.

"Good to see death hasn't mellowed you."

Miss Bessie glared at me. "I'm coming for you next, you know."

"I have no doubt," I sighed. "Just leave my underwear alone."

"Can I stay with you?" Bella asked Claire.

"Can. Stay. With. You," Claire's ghost app called out.

"Who's asking that?" Claire asked suspiciously. I could see the fear written across the woman's face that her charge would follow her even in death. "Who wants to know that?"

"Bella," I told her.

"Oh," she said with relief. "Of course, Bella. Petey and I would love it," she admitted and then bit her lip, worried. "Especially since I'm out of a job now."

"I left her some money," Miss Bessie told me. "She put up with me for years, she deserves it. You might want to tell her about it."

"Let's let it be a surprise," I whispered. Miss Bessie nodded. "Claire, when you feel up to it, come visit me. As much as I'm running around, maybe it would be a good idea to have someone at the shop full-time. Azalea's great, but she'll be in college soon, and I'm losing a lot of business." Once Miss Bessie turned her attention to me, no doubt I'd be losing even more, running all over town looking for old bottles.

"Not to mention all the psychic readings you'll be doing." Pepper handed me the day's morning paper. I grabbed it and looked.

"Oh, crap," I whispered. I was on the front page, my eyes rolled back in my head as I faked a psychic vision in the middle of a restaurant. The adjacent article outlined that Bella Grayson's murder would have never been cracked without my spontaneous psychic vision in Evangeline

Leroux's club the night before. "Oh, *crap*," I said again.

"My editor was having dinner there when it happened," Pepper said resentfully. "You're not allowed to do that kind of stuff without me there anymore. I *could* have had a front page byline."

"What's going to happen to Ella?" Ollie asked.

I flipped the paper open to the greyhound racing section. "Apparently, she's in the sixth race tonight," I told him. "Anyone want to place a bet?"

TWENTY-THREE

I couldn't help it.

Well, I probably could have if Pepper hadn't been so insistent that we had to watch Ella-Petey's first greyhound race.

But she was, and so here we were.

Besides, it was probably a good idea to get familiar with the track myself if Martin and I were going to be negotiating how to bring it all—well, the part that exploited dogs—to an end.

"I think that she's just going to sit there when that gate opens and not move," Pepper said as we wound our way through the crowd. "Or she'll run the wrong way. Or she'll try and escape."

"She did say it was just running in a circle, and any idiot could do it." I craned my neck to find a couple of chairs. "I guess we're about to see that theory tested."

"Miss Delphi," a deep voice boomed from a small crowd gathered at the entrance to the private suites. As the clustered gathering opened up, I spotted Martin and Jeeves talking with Detective Conroe and Chief Clutterbuck. "Why don't you join us?" the chief called, holding up a foamy pint of beer. Martin looked uncomfortable. Jeeves looked like...well, Jeeves.

"I've *always* wanted to sit in those luxury boxes, Fortuna," Pepper whispered fiercely at me. "Don't you dare say no. Oh, and they could say something that would give us information for a story. But mostly," she nodded quickly, "I really want to watch the race in the luxury box."

"Chief Clutterbuck," I called and waved as we moved toward them. "Gentlemen," I nodded as we stepped into their circle. "We appreciate the invitation, thank you. Pepper's quite interested in seeing what life is like in one of those suites."

I don't know what she's doing here, Martin, Jeeves responded telepathically to his boss. *Perhaps she simply came to see the dog race out of curiosity. Hold it together.*

Martin glared at me.

I met his gaze steadily.

"The suites are quite nice and much quieter

than down here in the hallway." Chief Clutterbuck extended his arm up the stairs and smiled at me. "Shall we?"

* * *

It didn't take long for Clutterbuck to corner me far away from the rest of the group.

"Miss Delphi, do you mind if I ask you a question?"

"You can ask me anything you want, Chief," I answered politely. Turning, I smiled. "I reserve the right to not answer until I have a lawyer present, but you can ask anything you want."

Clutterbuck stepped back and cocked his head, examining me. His expression said that he was mostly sure that I'd cracked a joke, but he wasn't *entirely* sure I was trying to be funny. "I wanted to ask you about your vision of the murder weapon," he said, lowering his voice. "Now, since the newspaper claimed witness to your little psychic episode, I have to—for the department's reputation —support your claimed version of events. But I'm profoundly curious."

"Curious about what, sir?"

"How you knew where the hypodermic needle was." It didn't sound like a question.

"You know as much as I do, Chief Clutterbuck.

I don't know where the visions come from." I turned away and grabbed a bottle of water from an ice chest on the side of the open-air room. "I don't even know why I said what I said, really."

"Is that so." Again, didn't sound like a question.

"It is." I turned back and smiled up at him.

Chief Clutterbuck's stare was as penetrating as Martin's could be. I wondered if there was an alpha male class where they all learned the art of staring at people like they were prey about to be eaten by a wolf. There was only cold calculation in him—as if he was trying to determine how far he could push me.

"I've known Jeff Abernathy for years. Years and years," he told me, holding my gaze. "Now, I can't say that I'm surprised he pulled what he pulled. The man likes money, and he's had a rough go of it of late." Clutterbuck folded his arms. "I am surprised, however, that he would rush to the police station to take responsibility for it."

"Confession's good for the soul," I shrugged. "Maybe he just felt guilty."

"He knew his son had caused Spike's death, and he never felt guilty," Clutterbuck countered. "I find it hard to believe he just developed a conscience out of thin air, Miss Delphi."

"What are you asking me, Chief Clutterbuck?" I asked him outright.

"I just wondered if you knew anything about his sudden change of morality, that's all," the tall man asked, leaning in. I stepped back, and Jeeves shot a concerned glance from across the room where he and Martin were listening to Pepper. "Or if you had anything to do with it."

"How could I have had anything to do with it?" I asked, and checked the time on my phone just to break the head cop's uncomfortable stare.

"Well, I don't know, Ms. Delphi," Clutterbuck responded. "But your friend over there seems to think you have a lot of crazy supernatural powers. I've read her blog. Well, before she removed everything about you—at your request, no doubt." He nodded toward Pepper. "Like I said, I've known Jeff for years. That confession? That wasn't like him."

"I have some telepathic ability, Chief, that's all," I told him. While that was a lie, it was true that I had absolutely nothing to do with Jeff Abernathy's change of heart. "I can't change someone's personality overnight. I think your friend just couldn't live with what he did, that's all."

"So, since you have such a great psychic ability, can you find missing people?" he asked, his tone and expression changing completely. "We certainly would like to make an arrest in Bella Grayson's case, and would love it if you had any insight as to where Ella might be."

"No idea, sir," I lied again.

Clutterbuck made no reply. He just stared at me.

"So, now I have a question."

"Yes, ma'am." He nodded.

"Yesterday morning, you were practically hostile toward me. I believe you said you would enjoy seeing my...oh, what was it...oh, that's right. My *tight little hippie ass* in jail. Now, you've invited me into a luxury suite for a chat." He smiled warmly, throwing me. "What changed?"

"Why, Miss, Delphi, I thought you said you were psychic," Clutterbuck chuckled. "Don't you know?"

With that, he turned on his heel and walked toward the back—leaving me baffled.

* * *

The gates opened, and Ella-Petey never made it out of the gate.

"Well, that answers that question," Pepper muttered, disappointed.

"I still can't figure out why on earth Clutterbuck's suddenly nice to me."

"Because you may be useful to him," Jeeves said

as he came up beside us. The three of us watched silently as Hoyt Abernathy lead the terrified Ella-Petey toward the back on a lead. He handled the frightened animal with surprising gentleness. "The whole town knows that you helped the police uncover a murder that had gone unidentified."

"I didn't, though. I mean, I helped, but it was really Ollie that realized what was happening."

"You made Clutterbuck look good."

Pepper nodded at Jeeves's statement. "And it sounds to me like he thinks you may have more powers than just the fortune-telling," she added. "Maybe he's worried you'll fidget-finger him and make him start confessing all his sins, too."

"But I had nothing to do with that."

"But he doesn't know that," Jeeves pointed out. "He hasn't beaten you yet, so maybe it's just a change in tactics."

I snorted. "Keep your enemies closer?"

"Something like that," he responded quietly.

I turned and stared. "Is that what you're doing?"

"I don't think we're enemies," Jeeves said as Pepper's eyes widened. Announcing loudly that she needed more shrimp, she slipped away toward the buffet in the back of the suite. "I don't blame you for calling Martin to the mat on the greyhound racing. He does want something from you, and you have an opportunity to get something you want."

I let out a breath. "You make it sound so sordid."

"Isn't it?" Jeeves raised an eyebrow. "You're offering to trade imprisoned spirits for imprisoned animals. Using suffering beings as leverage. That's pretty sordid."

"Except I didn't imprison anyone, and I still need to do some work on figuring out just what's in those bottles. I don't know for sure it's the witches, and I don't know for sure they're suffering." I pointed down to the track. "I know for sure they are."

"Well," Jeeves finally replied, "I don't have an argument for that."

"I'm sure Martin would."

"Martin is quite shocked at the turn of events, yes," the vampire nodded. "And he does care about you a great deal, so that's making the situation... emotionally complicated for him."

Just then, Evangeline Laroux slinked in and wrapped herself around Martin with a coo and a kiss on the cheek. Her father nodded and seemed unconcerned that his daughter wouldn't have looked out of place in a high-end brothel in Las Vegas.

"Oh, yeah," I jerked my head toward the two. "Looks real complicated."

"You don't know everything."

"You don't tell me everything," I pointed out.

Jeeves and I exchanged glances. What do you say once you establish that secrets are being kept, and they will continue to be maintained? Not a damn thing.

"You'll contact me when you're ready to outline how this will work?" he asked me. I nodded. "Good. I'll do my best to keep Martin from badgering you, but please don't take too long. This is his mother we're talking about. He's not always...rational when it comes to this endeavor."

I nodded, and the handsome vampire left me alone.

* * *

As I cuddled up with Gideon in bed, I realized my list of things to handle was growing longer.

I needed to rev up my work with Miss Bessie and confirm her stories of this town.

I needed to work more intently with the magic book.

I needed to come up with a plan to shut down greyhound racing that moved fast enough to solve the issue, but slow enough so that I wasn't racing around throwing bottles against trees.

I had to train Claire to help out in the shop.

I had to figure out how I turned Ella into a dog, so I could turn her back. I couldn't leave her as a greyhound forever...right? No, no, I couldn't do that.

Well, she is a murderer...

No, I needed to change her back.

Gideon sent an image of me, with my eyes closed.

"You're right, Gideon," I told him, squeezing him close. "Tomorrow's another day."

And in a town like Mystic's End, that day could bring just about anything.

THANK YOU FOR READING!
I hope you enjoyed The Greyt Escape! Please think about leaving a review! Fortuna and Gideon's adventures continue in Book 6, Boozehounds and Ball Drops!

AFTERWORD

This fictional book has focused on the very real plight of greyhounds within greyhound racing. While much work has been done to end the suffering and exploitation of these wonderful dogs, much more work still needs to be done.

GREY2K USA Worldwide is a non-profit 501(c)4 advocacy organization located at 7 Central Street, Arlington, Massachusetts 02476. 100% of donations support their mission to end dog racing, pass greyhound protection laws and promote greyhound adoption.

For more information on their work, to make a donation, or to get involved, visit https://www. grey2kusa.org/

KEEP UP WITH LEANNE LEEDS

Thanks so much for reading! I hope you liked it! Want to keep up with me?

Visit leanneleeds.com to:

Find all my books...

Sign up for my newsletter...

Like me on Facebook...

Follow me on Twitter...

Follow me on Instagram...

Thanks again for reading!

Leanne Leeds

FIND A TYPO? LET US KNOW!

Typos happen. It's sad, but true.

Though we go over the manuscript multiple times, have editors, have beta readers, and advance readers it's inevitable that determined typos and mistakes sometimes find their way into a published book.

Did you find one? If you did, think about reporting it on leanneleeds.com so we can get it corrected.

www.ingramcontent.com/pod-product-compliance
Lightning Source LLC
Chambersburg PA
CBHW031548240626
47153CB00002B/423